Leigh Jenkins

(Volume 1)

ARJUN

First Published in 2021

Becomeshakespeare.com

One Point Six Technologies Pvt Ltd
123, Building J2, Shram Seva Premises, Wadala Truck Depot,
Wadala (East), Mumbai 400037, India
T: +91 8080226699

Wordit Art Fund helps deserving authors publish their work by providing monetary support. To apply for funding, please visit us at www.BecomeShakespeare.com

ISBN - 978-93-5438-857-6

About the Author

Atharva Rajesh Joshi is from Pune. He likes to read thrillers, especially murder mysteries. His love for crime fiction rose after reading stories of great writers like Agatha Christie and Arthur Conan Doyle. After reading many of such stories he had an idea of writing about a detective who apart from solving crimes shows more about his personal life too. So he started writing about this detective called Leigh Jenkins.

Apart from reading books, he likes to read and write poems. From the day he started writing poems till now he has a collection of one hundred and seventeen poems. Atharva uses the term 'ARjun' as his pen name. The word has a Sanskrit origin and it means brightness and clarity. He believes that his writing is bright and clear hence uses the name `ARjun`.

CONTENTS

Chapter 1

Disappearance of the Grail.

It was a holiday for private detective Leigh Charles Jenkins. The time was almost quarter to nine,when his bell rang. He was one of the most famous and cunning detective in London. Jenkins was a man with an average height of five feet and six inches, had a completely muscular and well maintained physique. A clean face with brown eyes and long blonde hair made him more attractive. He was a man of his word, a gentleman and the favorite person of the people in Scotland Yard. But most important of all, a man of his values he was. Ladies liked him because of his charming look and his flirtatious nature. People in the yard were his fans because he was the perfect detective.

Jenkins opened the door. There was a brown haired man with blue eyes and a short slim moustache. "Hello Vic", said Jenkins. "Hi Leigh" Goldenlod said.

Victor Goldenlod was the Senior Curator and Chief of the British Museum and the security chief of the Queen's private collection. A man passionate of history. "So come in and give me a shake" Said Jenkins. Goldenlod came in and gave Jenkins a handshake, and then he sat on the chair. Jenkins noticed something weird about his hands. "So is someone else expected?" Jenkins asked."Of course not" Victor said. "Well, then you are free to close my door."Jenkins said. Victor went towards the door and closed it. "Look at you Vic, at an age of 27 you are in charge of the Queen's private collection. While I being just 25 am a detective." Said Jenkins "Yeah Jenkins, I am not here to chit chat. I know,you are a detective,to whom Scotland yard praises. That's why I came to you."Said Victor. "I know Goldie, so what is gone from the private collection? Is it the Sword of the Indian King, 'the triumph of Caesar'? Oh no, wait, it is the Grail, right?" Said Jenkins."How do you know?" Victor asked. "The newspaper obviously, Vic" Said Jenkins.

"The Grail has not left the Museum. That is for sure." Victor said "How are you so sure?" Jenkins asked. "You see all the relics and artifacts have a tag fitted on them. A light glows in the control room when a particular artifact crosses the radius of the museum. The light that belongs to the Grail is not up yet" Victor explained. "Okay fine Victor ,I will help you find the relic" said Jenkins."A special chamber inspired by Leonardo's 'The Last supper' was constructed for the display of the Grail. The Grail was brought here from Spain for display." Said Goldenlod. "Alright Vic. Let's go and find it." Said Jenkins. "Yes, I know we can find it, we can right?" Goldenlod asked with a bit tensed face. "Don't worry, Vic. I'll do whatever I can. Now let's get going" said Jenkins. They started for the museum without wasting any more time.

The Museum was like an aesthetic old man. Wise, filled with knowledge and some important relics, artifacts were displayed. One could really feel history. Without wasting anytime, they directly went to the room where Royal collection was displayed. Beside the door to the royal collection there was a counter on which, stood a girl. Jenkins caught a sweet scent. The girl was probably between twenty five or twenty six. She was wearing a staff blazer and a white shirt under it. Her fair complexion a pair of streamlined small lips with a maroon lipstick applied on them and a small curved nose, deep sea blue eyeballs and short black hair made her look very gorgeous. Jenkins looked at her; he noticed something strange about her hair. "She is Miss scarlet Fox. The secretary of the royal collection."Goldenlod said. "Fascinating" Jenkins remarked. Victor Goldenlod introduced Jenkins to the whole staff of the royal collection. Though some of them weren't present, as they were in the surveillance room. "So Miss. Fox, can you show me the place where the Grail was kept." Jenkins asked. "Sure, follow me Mister Detective." She said. "Oh please, call me Leigh." Said Jenkins. "Then call me Scarlett." She said. Victor gave him a look. "So,Miss ,oh.. I mean Scarlett. Lead the way" said Jenkins. Scarlett and Jenkins went inside, while Victor accompanied them to the chamber, where the Grail was kept before it was stolen. The chamber was a complete three dimensional replica of Da Vinci's "The Last Supper" Lord Jesus, the apostles Judas Iscariot, James the great, Simon the zealot. Every single statue was made with brilliance. The Holy Grail was not at its place. Jenkins made a round of the whole setup. There was a jug which resembled a flower vase kept on the dining table. "Is this flower vase a part of the last supper?" asked Jenkins. "How did this jug come on the table" Said Goldenlod. "So, it's usually not on the dining table?" Asked Jenkins. "Yes, it was always kept down there, the chamber was not tampered since robbery. So how on the earth did the jug came up?" Goldenlod said with an expression of fear and anxiety. "Fascinating very,very fascinating" said Jenkins "I want every corner of the chamber photographed and some photographs of the chamber before the robbery."Jenkins ordered. "Okay, I am sensing trouble here Jenkins." said Goldenlod. "So can I get the whole surveillance footage of the chamber of last night, Scarlett?" asked Jenkins. "Of course you can" said Scarlett.

A girl stressed and tensed came rushing towards the chamber. Meanwhile all three of them were out of the chamber. The girl cried "Mr.Goldenlod there is a situation here" "Tell me Gwen, what you got.Oh Iam sorry,Jenkins this is Gwen Radcliffe,the head of our surveillance and technical analysis,also a journalism expert." Said Victor. Gwen Radcliffe stood five feet five inches,she had blonde hair and a fair complexion. Her hair were straightened, her nose was small which perfectly suited her face, small lips with a red lipstick applied on it. Most importantly her green deep eye balls and eyebrows sharp at the end made her look beautiful. She looked at Jenkins. "Well Miss Radcliffe you had a situation dint you" Goldenlod asked. "Oh yes, I was going through the surveillance when I saw that the cameras had stopped recording for an hour yesterday night, and the laser tag inside which the chalice was kept was also disabled." She said. "Can you tell me the time when the cameras and the lasers were disabled" He asked. "It was night 10.39 pm to 11.40 pm." She answered. "Then why did we not get to know immediately, if I'm not wrong Eric, John and Scott were on night surveillance," Said goldenlod. "Yes, sir you are right I think we should interrogate them." Said Gwen. "She is right. I want all three of them here right now." Said Jenkins, "I will get them to you, and Gwen will go bring the attendance records." Said Scarlett. It was 2.45 when John Smith entered the room. He was tall and handsome man,with black hair and a small nineties type moustache. He had dark brown eyeballs and a square head .He was wearing a staff blazer and a shirt beneath it."So how long have you been working here Mr.Smith? Jenkins asked. "Not more than two years." He said. "What do you do here and is it okay if I called you John?" Leigh asked "Oh I work here as a night shift observer and in day I work as the security of the royal collection. Sure you may call me John." He said. "So tell me John ,were you working last night?" "Yes he was" said Goldenlod. "I saw him myself." "Oh shut it victor. Let me play the detective here. Oh well actually I am the detective here." Jenkins said. "Okay, okay I will be quite." Jenkins continued asking questions. "Tell me John what you were doing last night, between 10.30pm to 12 am? "Well that is quite a much time. My duty was finished at 10.00pm itself and it was the time for Eric and Scott's duty" He said. "Okay, Victor just do me a thing, bring last night's leaving records and check Mr. Smith's entry. Smith shouted in anger "You don't trust me puny detective do you!" "Calm down John, I am in the seat where I can trust no one" said Jenkins. "Whatever" said John. "Okay thank you for giving your time, now can you please send Mr. Scott inside?" Jenkins asked. "Okay fine,Smith left the room. "So what do you think of him Jen? Has he done it?" Said Goldenlod. "I don't think so" Said Jenkins. "How can you say so?" he asked. "My dear Goldenlod there are two types of people, the ones who have committed a crime and the ones which haven't .The ones which do, carry it in their eyes.Then there is the third type, like me who can see in their eyes like none can." Said Jenkins "Well that doesn't explain that he is the thief or not."Said Goldenlod "We will see that when the records come." Said Jenkins. He can steal the Grail can't he?" Asked Goldenlod. "He can, but " Jenkins said. "But what"Goldenlod asked. "But he seemed an impatient guy. As you said this morning, the Grail has not left the building.So if he had to do it,he would have done it last night and would have sold it last night itself." Jenkins said. "And why may that be?" asked Goldenlod. See last night was an electricity breach in whole London for two hours.This was from 10.30pm to 12.30am.This could be the reason for the cameras and lasers to stop working. So the Grail was definitely stolen in that time. Yesterday was Friday 22nd , so the black market was active and adding to it, yesterday was also the Comissioner's birthday. So police activities were very less yesterday. It's a Tradition of the yard that officers will do only half of the duty whenever it's a higher up's birth day. Weird tradition right? So if he would have wanted to sell it at a huge price, he would have done it yesterday itself."Jenkins said in a breath. Goldenlod nodded. "So Smith is out of question." Said goldenlod. Jenkins nodded. There was a knock on the door. "Come in" said Goldenlod. Scott Atkin entered the room at sharp 3.10pm. He was a shabby man. An oval face and French cut beard,pair of deep darkened lips and some hair on his head constructed his face. But had a muscular body. 'There might be a chance he might be a heavy smoker, and oh my god this smell of tobacco will kill me off' Jenkins thought. "I do not like your face" said Jenkins. "Excuse me!" Said Scott. As he opened his mouth, the intensity of the tobacco odor in the air raised. Some time passed in normal questions. "So, apart from here, do you work anywhere else?" Jenkins asked. "I work at LESC for just three days in a week." He said. Jenkins could not tolerate the odor and his ugly face so he came directly on the point. "Now, tell me Scott, What did you do when the cameras and laser tag were disabled last night?" He said. "Oh, did anything like that happen last night, because I left home early at 10." He said. "Is that your regular time?" Jenkins asked. "Nope, I was feeling drowsy last night I wanted to sleep early so I asked Eric to look at my screen and I left." Said Scott. "Did anyone see you going?" Jenkins asked. "I recorded my departure time in that biometric device." He said. "So what were you doing between 10.30 to 12.00 pm" He asked. "Sleeping" Said Scott. "Alright Scott you can go now and please send Eric inside." Said Jenkins. Scott left.

A moment later Gwen arrived with the records. "Where is Eric?" Jenkins asked. "Scar, Scarlett is looking for him" Gwen said. "Alright we will interrogate you first." Victor Said. Both started to interrogate her. First some random questions were asked to her. She seemed quite unstable and restless."Tell me Miss Radcliffe how long have you worked here?" "It's been seven months I work here. Mr.Jensen." Who's Jensen?" asked Goldenlod "err I mean Jenkins." "Hmm" said Goldenlod." Tell me Gwen what time you leave from work?" asked Jenkins." I leave at 6.30 everyday, but yesterday I packed early at 5." "Okay, can you tell me what you were doing last night from 10.30 to

12." Asked Jenkins." I was ,I was er, having a date. " With whom?" asked Goldenlod."With" she was about to say when a sudden knock disturbed the interrogation. "Come in" said Goldenlod with an expression of anger mixed with dissatisfaction. The door opened and Scarlett came in "there is something you need to see Leigh and well you too Mr.Goldenlod." Said Scarlett. It was almost 4.45pm, "What is it about?" asked Goldenlod. " Its about Eric" said Scarlett. "I am telling you Jenkins this Eric Londoner is the key." "Perhaps he was, would be the correct word here." Said Scarlett. "What do you mean?"Asked Goldenlod. "Fascinating." Said Jenkins. Goldenlod gave a questioning look to Jenkins. "What is it, will you tell me Miss Scarlett Fox." "Eric is found dead Sir,in the canteen." Said Scarlett. " What! " said Goldenlod.

"Is anyone here a doctor?" Asked Jenkins to the whole staff.A man stood and said. "Yes I was a trained doctor,but I don't practice anymore." The man was in his fifties had grey hair and a well maintained proper English moustache. He was a six feet tall man with a well maintained physique. Okay sir may I know your name please?" "I am Dr. Harris Clark." "a moment with you Victor." Said Jenkins. "what is it Leigh?" asked Goldenlod. "I think we might require this guy,for checking the body" " you are trusting a random person aren't you Jenkins,what if he has killed him." "Well you leave everything to me Victor; I know what Iam doing." "Fine" said Goldenlod. Jenkins went to the doctor and asked him to accompany them. The doctor agreed. Eric Londoner's body was lying on the chair in the corner of the canteen facing back to the door.There were two tea cups on the table,one that was close to Eric,and the other was close to the opposite chair of Eric. He seemed a five feet six inches and was a red head.He had no facial hair.And was about 27 to 28.There was a knife in his back which could be the reason of his death. "tell me Doc what you got there?" asked Jenkins. "Our victim here was stabbed in the back,and yes he was stabbed when he was unconscious.So he was not able to defend himself. I can't say that the murderer was a male or a female, because he was stabbed from a very close distance,though the wound is deep could have been the effort of a man but a women can also have such strength when she is so close.And the person who has stabbed him has good information, and is the master in locating interior organs.As the knife is stabbed so precisely,that it has ripped a hole from the center of the heart.The killer could be a doctor or an anatomy expert.And most important of all the victim has died five hours ago that means he died precisely at 3.00pm." "How could that be,the blood still hasn't dried.It might be hardly an hour to his death." Jenkins bent down and dipped his finger in the stream of blood and said." Fascinating very fascinating." The body was going to be covered so Jenkins had a last look at it; he saw a small dried stream of blood coming out of his mouth and some redness on his neck.He touched the throat; while the whole body was cold the throat still was warm.He just noticed a chit of paper in his hand stained with blood. He kept the chit in his pocket.The body was covered and kept aside. Jenkins,Goldenlod,Gwen,Scarlett,Scott,John and Dr.Clark were in the canteen." Well this is now becoming worse,first the robbery of the Grail,and now Eric's murder."said John." Yes,Eric was my friend,a good understanding friend." Said Gwen. "Yes he was a nice man, oh Eric ." said Goldenlod. " I did not know him well,but I never thought that I will have to see a colleague's dead body." Said the doctor. Gwen was in tears. "May his soul rest in peace" everyone said together."Okay everyone,I want to interrogate you people once again." Said Jenkins. "Whom to start with?"Goldenlod asked. "No, Now I am going to interrogate all of them at one time. By the way Victor, wasn't there anyone in the canteen who might have seen Eric?" Jenkins asked. "No Jen, The whole staff was in the reception except Scott and Eric. The chefs in the canteen only come thrice a week, they weren't here yesterday. Only the coffee guy came and made coffee in the morning, after him no one has gone in the canteen." Goldenlod said. "Alright Vic, now everybody stand in a line and answer the questions one by one that I am going to ask you." Jenkins said. Everybody formed a line. "Alright now, tell me one by one, who was doing what between 2.15 to 3.15.?" He asked. Well I was outside the conference room with everyone else." Said Dr.Clark. "At precisely 2.45 I went to the attendance and biometrics room for collecting the records,it took a bit time for the records to get printed. But it was done till" said Gwen. "What about you Mr.Smith. " Well I was with you.In the conference room,you were asking me questions,I was accused for nothing ." "That's enough John!" Goldenlod said. "Now I think that you are the one who stole the chalice and you are the one who killed Eric." "No! I'm telling you a hundred times that I haven't stolen anything neither I have killed anyone." "Oh whatever." "Well calm down both of you!" ordered Jenkins." And that is enough Mr.Smith.Calm down Goldie. Okay ,what about you Scarlett." "I offered a juice to Gwen then she said that she was in the attendance and biometrics room for the records,she told me to look for the three men.Which exactly I was doing." Until I found the two of them.Then I went to find Eric.And eventally I got to know that,he had died.Then I came and told you about it." "Okay so what were you doing Mr.Atkin" asked Jenkins. "I came to be interrogated at precisely 3.10pm. I was in the other section of the museum between 2.45 to 3.00 ,so Scarlett came and told me about the interrogation,and then I rushed here." " Okay" said Jenkins. "Now I want everyone out except Gwen." Everyone left while Gwen was inside. "Can you tell me at what time did you get the records?" "Well I got them at ten minutes to 3." "Then please tell me what you were doing between 2.50 to 3.30?" asked Jenkins. "I.. err...,I don't really remember." "Well guess what, I do remember between 2.50 and 3.30 you were killing Eric Londoner." Said Goldenlod. Gwen said "I did not kill him.Please trust me. I really don't remember." "Okay Gwen,let it be, hey do you guys have lockers here.Because its getting a bit warm,I want to remove my trench coat.Can you show me the locker space Gwen?" Asked Jenkins. "Sure" she said.Both were going to the Locker hall. "So Gwen tell me how was Eric anyhow?" asked Jenkins.Gwen seemed little depressed she said " He was good, he was really very good,a good colleague and an excellent man" " Was he married?" asked Jenkins." He wasn't she said. They reached the locker hall." Can you show me Scarlett's Locker. I would like to keep it there," "That's there,No 2294." Jenkins went towards the locker "Its locked,can I use yours? Asked Jenkins "sure its 2234" Jenkins opened the locker.They saw a packet of betel and something special very, very special. "Oh my god! I did not do it, how did it come here, how on the earth did it come here." Gwen was in complete shock, she collapsed. Jenkins called Dr. Clark. He was thinking something desperately. Everyone gathered in front of the chamber of the Grail. Goldenlod asked "well did you come to a conclusion Jenkins if not then,do it fast." "Can you take me to a cold place?" Asked Jenkins. Golednlod and Jenkins went in a cooler section. "Okay so just leave me alone for some time Goldie,just gather everyone outside. Because it is going to be fascinating ,very very fascinating". Jenkins locked himself inside that chamber. He was standing before the sword of a mighty warrior. Then he sat down on a chair while Goldenlod brought the whole staff outside the chamber. "What is it now? Are we going to get interrogated again?" John asked "Keep patience John." Said Goldenlod. "Is he inside?" The doctor asked "Yes he is" answered Goldenlod. "So did he find the killer,did he find the Grail?" asked Scarlett, "No not yet,I don't know." Said Goldenlod.

Inside the chamber,Jenkins started talking to himself. 'So ladies and gentlemen,what do we have here. Well one: wine glass of great importance and worth millions of Euros that is stolen. Two: the flower vase like structure that is always kept down on the left of the dining table that comes up.Three:the interrogation of all the suspects. Four: a suspect that is murdered.Five:A box of betel in the locker of a girl who doesn't consume it at all. Okay.

Outside the room goldenlod started to think.First he started to stare at John,he started thinking. 'Did he do it,no he did not,and also he is a good friend of Eric.He hasn't done it.' Then he stared at Atkin. 'Is it a possibility that he might have stolen it and killed Eric? Yes he could've ,but no just look at him, he hasn't .He does not have the strength to do so.' Then he started to stare at Scarlett. 'Well did she do it? It can be,okay it cannot be.She looks so confident and innocent.Plus she has an alibi.She has not done it.' Then started staring at the doctor.' There is a high chance he might have done it.He analyzed the body,how was he so sure.That means he might have done it.But no,he seems an ethical person he has not done it too.' Just then Gwen arrived.Goldenlod started to stare her.

While, inside the room. Jenkins was talking to himself. ' So there is something that is not being caught,but what? Hmm.The sixth thing the victim's surname.What does that bring me?Fascinating .Seven:Gwen was hesitating to speak during the first interrogation.Well was she afraid? No she wasn't. She wasn't hesistating .she was not aware of her surroundings. Well was she hallucinating? she isn't a drug addict. Then why were her eyes reddened. Eight: why were there red marks on the dead's throat? Well there were three glasses on the table, one which the victim drank half. The other two were finished. Wait, what does that mean.

Outside Goldenlod was staring at Gwen. 'She is looking suspicious from the morning,she is even behaving weird. She was even hesitating to answer questions during the interrogation.Okay she doesn't even have an alibi.Well this is it.She is the one.She has killed Eric,and then she only must have stolen the grail.Yes this is it.I have solved a mystery myself.'

A long time had passed and everyone seemed irritated. Just then the door opened and Jenkins came out.As he came out,there was a silence of some seconds and then,everybody pounced on him with question. " Did you find the chalice?" Asked Goldenlod." Did you figure out who is the murderer?" asked the doctor." Who killed Eric?" asked John." Did you get to conclusion?" asked Scott." He has solved everything hasn't he?" said Scarlett.

In all this fuss Gwen was silent. Jenkins said, "everybody come inside.I have something that has to be announced." Everyone followed him inside. Then they started looking curiously at him.

"It was my holiday today, when my old mate vic came and blew it to ashes. However anything for Victor. I came here at this place which smells out history. This particular case was interesting. My mind started to think about all the complex solutions as it could." He removed a blood stained chit and continued "This was found in Mr. Eric's pocket. A chit with two codes" said Jenkins. "What codes?" Goldenlod asked. "Locker numbers mate. These locker codes took me to the procedure of the hiding the grail properly. Ladies and gentlemen, now to be honest and clear there is not a thief but there was a team of thieves. The first member was supposed to sit in the surveillance room to cover the other two members. The second was supposed to open the chamber of the section and the third agile and sleek was supposed to get the grail out. But our agile person was scared and committed that one mistake which has lead to their unmasking. The main thief who went in to get the grail by mistake kicked that vase on the corner of that dining table. And then the vase which always stood down beside the leg of the table came up on the corner. This was a major mistake. But why up? The thief could have kept it down as it was. This is an aesthetic of a woman. Agile and sleek she might be but she committed the robbery in haste. And who is the person always worried, in a hurry and acts wierd?" he said,Goldenlod cut him and said "its Gwen, yes it has to be her." Gwen panicked "No, I could never do such thing." She said. "I haven't finished yet" Leigh shouted. Everybody looked at him curiously. "Now, one of the robbers knew that electricity would be cut off for sometime in this area. Therefore chose yesterday. Ladies and gentlemen our little team of robbers is" everyone sharpened their ears, Gwen started breathing heavily. "Eric Londoner, Scott Atkin and the one and only Miss Scarlett Fox" Jenkins said with a smile. "What, this is impossible, are you out of your mind?" Said Scott. While Scarlett was silent. "Scott, you served as a medical assistant in a hospital and then as an assistant in a drug store. You have good knowledge of human anatomy. Well working at the drug store taught you about effects of drugs and how to use them. Then you said you work part time at LESC, well what is that, London Electricity Supply Corp. So you knew about the short time supply cut. Then Eric, his job was just to take every one off the board by sending them home. You opened the door and Scarlett went inside. She took the Holy Grail and while taking it she kicked the vase by mistake. Well there is crack on the vase. Then she hid the Grail in Scott's locker for the time being. You knew that lockers would be checked the next day. Today while checking of the lockers you took it and hid it in Gwen's locker after the checking was done. So even if the Grail was found a direct suspension would fall on Gwen. "But Leigh, Gwen was acting weird all the time. You can't ignore that." Victor said "Oh yes that brings me to how the murder was committed. Eric was blackmailing both of them for maybe a larger share of money. When I arrived they knew that Eric would spill off everything. So they killed him. And yes Doctor Clark, he was Stabbed yes, but before that he was cyanided. Then he was stabbed to misguide us. They wanted us to think that he was stabbed so again suspicion would go on Gwen. But no Gwen literally had an alibi. She acted unnaturally because she was drugged with a heavy dose of LSD as it makes the consumer hallucinate quickly. So during the interrogation she was hallucinating. Now you have your robbers and murderers." Said Leigh. Everyone took a deep breath of relief except the sinners. "Did you do, what I told you to do Victor?" Jenkins asked. "Sure I did, like the last time." Victor said and opened the door. Some cops came in. "Here, kind people, here are the sinners who committed murder and the cheapest sin of stealing such holy and pure artifact." Jenkins remarked.

"Let's arrest the murderers" said the police captain. She was about to handcuff Scarlett, just then Scarlett removed a knife. Scott pulled a revolver from his hand and pulled Gwen towards him. He put the revolver on her head. "If any one tries to arrest me, I shoot her" he said. Just then the captain sprinted towards Scarlett and kicked on her hand. The knife fell down.

Scott fired in the air. "Don't even think about me" He said. Jenkins looked at Gwen and raised his eyebrow. Gwen slithered her hand in her pocket and slowly removed a pen. Jenkins raised his eyebrow again. With all force in her body Gwen stabbed the pen in Scott`s leg. He shouted miserably. Jenkins pounced and punched on his face. The revolver went flying and Scott was on the ground. Jenkins then looked at the spot of tobacco on his fist "Tch, disgusting" he said.

After some time the criminals were arrested and statements were taken. "You have saved me again Jen" said Victor. "Anything for you Goldenlod, well there is something more to save" Said Jenkins. He went towards Gwen. "That was something great you did back in there

Mr. Jenkins." She said. "That is my expertise." He said. "You really are a good detective" She said. "Well, Miss. Radcliffe, are you alright now?" He asked by comforting her. "I am alright" She said. "Would you like a cup of coffee?" Jenkins asked. "I know a place nearby" She said.

Chapter 2

Close Relations.

1996. king`s shore drive, little port, London "Oh slow her down Spen, you are pushing it too hard" said Karla. "No darling, I totally have her in control. Alas your brother worked on the breaks. So we have no worry, let the damn accelerator strike!" Spencer said. And suddenly!..

Museum Cafe London, two people were coming down the stairs when a police officer came running towards them. "Excuse me; I am looking for private detective Leigh Charles Jenkins." The officer said. "He is on a holiday" said blonde haired man wearing brown leather trench coat. "You are the one aren't you" said the officer. "What is it?" Jenkins asked "There is a body found on the little port sir, we require you immediately." He said. "Who`s in charge?" asked Jenkins. "Robeerto King's man, sir" said the officer. "Is old man Robeerto in trouble again." Thought Jenkins. "Gwen, I am afraid we cannot carry on with our dinner plan, you care to join me later on some other day?" Jenkins asked to the girl with him. "Oh!, no problem Leigh. I`ll be looking forward to it." Gwen said. "Alright, but do send me a voice message when you get home" ordered Jenkins. "Alright said Gwen. "So Andrew Bridge, take me to the crime scene." Jenkins ordered "I did not tell you my name sir, neither I am wearing my name tag, sir" said Andrew. "Look Andrew, I have worked with Robeerto quite a few times, he said he is mentoring a trainee, but he didn't tell me the name. When last time I met him, I smelled a perfume, which I know doesn't belong to him. So when I asked him about it, he showed me the bottle, which said from Andrew Bridge. And the cigarette packet, you are keeping in your shirt pocket, says 'Lockart`s' that's the company that manufactures cigarettes as well as perfumes I assume." Jenkins said. "Y..Yes sir!" said Andrew. Then they went towards his car, and started towards little port. After an awkward silence, Andrew asked, "so what`s your qualification, sir?" "Oh, I did my graduation and post graduation in Law from Eastern University of London, and then a PhD in human psychology from Paris Descartes University." Said Jenkins. "I should call you Doctor then, shouldn't I?" said Andrew. "Oh, no need, I prefer the term 'Detective'" said Jenkins. "Understood" said Andrew. "Now tell me Andrew, why did you become a cop? Andrew had an expression of grief on his face. When he was just going to talk, Jenkins interrupted "So you lost some one, huh?" he said. Andrew`s mind travelled to his child hood. He started talking, "I was very close to my sister, let's say she was the only one who understood me. My father, not a great person but always had a grudge towards bad guys. He hated them. And was so merciless towards them. I don't really remember the year, I and my sister Jule, we wanted to see the Tower Bridge. So my father took us there in his car. It was a great day going. We had lunch in some nearby restaurant; you see I had affection towards puppies. I saw one near a corner of a building. So I immediately went to pet it. It saw me coming and went in the hollow between two buildings. And when I reached there, I saw something I never imagined I will. There was a bunch of, of child traffickers who were dealing a boy. And one of them saw me. They were coming for me, and I was so frozen on my feet. When just my sister arrived with my parents. My father took on all of the four goons who were there. We even rescued the boy, but those guys fled. We took the boy to the nearest police station. Well until night when we were returning home I was wondering I wanted to be a hero, like my father. That's what I was wondering. We reached home after an hour. And my mom told me to go bring some firewood from the shop, since we didn't have it at that moment. We all were so tired; we wanted to rest a bit. When I was going to the shop, I saw a black SUV parked near our house. I reached the shop, I took some firewood. And when I was near the house, the lights were on, on the first floor. And...." He stopped. His eyes were almost filled with tears. "Stop it, if you don't feel comfortable sharing this." Jenkins said. "No! This thing reminds me of my goal, it reminds me of the reason I joined the cops. So, my house`s door was opened already, I thought that Jule might have left it open while going to our back yard. I got inside..." tears started fumbling from his eyes. "There was a huge blot of blood on the wall corresponding to the door. And a few steps forward, my father`s body was lying and, without a head....... Somehow I managed to go towards the fire place in the hall, the hall was destroyed. And near the fireplace, my mom was lying. One bullet mark on her stomach, and another on her....he..head.... expecting something bad I tiptoed in horror towards mine and Jules`s room. When I opened the door, I saw Jule, unharmed but she was tied on a chair with a cloth stuffed in her mouth. I immediately ran towards her, but something, something was unnoticed in the room. Something dark, something destructive, which had already destroyed my family. When I was going towards her she tried shouting and nodding. I almost reached to her and, bang! Someone hit my head hard with a metal rod. The part corresponding to my left eye was bleeding. I fell down instantly. Wasn't able to see with my left eye. And vision started blurring from the right one. I heard a voice. 'Are we taking the boy too' said some one. 'No we aren't, boss was interested in the girl and we have finished the man who hit him hard.' And I fainted. After some hours when I opened my eyes, I found myself in a hospital. Mr.Logansan my neighbour was there with a police officer. The officer asked me some questions,kept a hand on my shoulder, and said. "Look boy, we will find those brats, the hell we will." But that police officer never turned up. He never caught those brats he was talking of. And that day, that day I decided, I decided to join the police. I want to end all the injustice that happens in this world." And then he had a tone of determination in his words, he continued. "And specially, I want to destroy that entire evil child trafficking organisations. The world is an unjustly place Mr. Jenkins, and no one cares about it. Everybody has their own cribbings. I want to see a peaceful place." He said. Jenkins was quiet satisfied listening to him. "Enough about my story. Tell me yours, I am sure you have one of your own" said Andrew. "My story huh?" said Jenkins. "Well as far as I remember, I don't have an interesting story either." He hesitated a bit, and said "lets save it for another time." He saw a board saying `little brink 1.5 miles'. Jenkins was a bit surprised seeing the board. It took him twenty years back, he started recollecting memories. Memories of hanging out with Annie and Ben. Jenkins wasn't a person who praised nostalgia, but a subtle smile struck him. "Oh hey, I know this place, I used to hang out here with my friends Annie and Ben, back when I was a kid." Said Jenkins. They reached the little brink after a couple of minutes. And Jenkins was in the mood of reliving his `after childhood` as he used to call it. All the fun, gossips and intense conversations, they used to have started running into his mind.

They both came out of the car; Jenkins saw a Grey headed man with really long grey moustaches. He was wearing a brown overcoat and a gun holsterwas hanging on his waist. He stood probably 5`6 long and had a proper maintained physique. But the most fascinating thing about him was, he was wearing sunglasses after the sun had set. The man shouted in excitement, "Ahh! Jenkin Kun, my boy. How do you do" Andrew was quite irritated because of that, but Jenkins went straight to the old man and hugged him. "So Robeerto san how was your trip to

Japan?" Asked Jenkins. "Ohh! I never told you about my trip to Japan did I?" Robeerto King's man asked Jenkins. "No, you did not." Said Jenkins "Then how do you know?" Robeerto asked. "First: You used the word 'Kun' it is a word for junior in Japanese. Tells me that you have lived a quite long there to adapt their tradition. Second: The snow monkey or the Japanese macaque brooch you are wearing on your coat, it's a shibuya product. That tells me, you have been trying to find it in nearly five to six Shibuya vending machines. Third: The Ishitakaya perfume you have put on your body, exclusively available at Shibuya shops in Tokyo. Tells me that you were in Tokyo." The detective said. "That was bloody brilliant!" Said Andrew. "That's nothing, stick with Jenkin Kun for some time and you will know what miracles he does." Said Robeerto. "Enough, I know you speak good Japanese oldie now stop calling me that. Will ya" said Jenkins. "Alright, alright I will call you what I used to, pretty boy." said Robeerto. "Whatever!" Jenkins said agitatedly. "Anyway, enough of chit chat, tell me what we got here?" Jenkins asked. "Take over, Bridge." Robeerto ordered. "Yes sir, so, we have a brown haired woman in her twenties, found dead by an old man who was passing by the stairs." Andrew said pointing towards a gate which had a board saying `Little Brink` which was leading to stairs. They went downwards from the gate, where they found two police officers. Seeing them there, Andrew was almost shocked. "Wait, where is the body gone, what are you two doing here! What the heck is going on?" he asked. The two officers weren't quite happy. While Jenkins`s nose had sensed something unexpected there. Jenkins looked down to the three stairs; there was huge blot of blood which wasn't completely dried yet. Then he directly stared in the eyes of one of the officer. After a couple of seconds, he stared in the eyes of the other one. He started thinking. `Both of these guys eyes are damn red, did they smoke marijuana, no it isn't possible, if it was then the part under their eyes should be darkened. It wasn't marijuana then, and what is this smell. Ohh wait don't tell me, the undried blot of blood tells me that the woman was murdered some hours ago. Okay so did these two guys dispose the body off? No, no. Well wait there are dragging marks in the grass. So if they did it, then they could have just carried the body. And according to Mr. Bridge, she was in her mid-twenties, about my age. So she mustn't be that bulkier. That means the person who dragged her might be ten years younger than her. No wait why would a mere 15 or 16 year old kill someone. No, so our murderer....amm, okay got it. And the body. Alright got it. ` "Answer me brats, where is the body?" shouted Andrew. "It was very cold out here, so I went at some distance to smoke." The first officer said. "What an idiot." Said Andrew. "And what about you, your majesty?" Andrew asked to the second. "I...a...I went to the car, to take a sh...shot." said the second officer. "Oh really, then where the hell is the bottle? You nugget" said Andrew. "Wait Bridge, they might not be lying." Said Jenkins. "How, these brats..." Andrew said angrily. "Relax boy, I think we leave this to the detective. All yours Leigh." Said Roberto. "Oh, that's so nice of you Oldie. Anyway, you guys see those drag marks." Said Jenkins pointing towards the drag marks in the grass. "Yes" Said everyone. "Let's find the body then." Ordered Jenkins. They started to follow the trail of the marks. At first the trail was in the dried grass, but as they were going diagonally towards the tributary the grass started to turn green. They instantly reached to the bank of the river, when they noticed a large pillar away from the bank which was supporting a bridge. Jenkins noticed a ray of light. And he guessed it to be a flash light. He whispered. "Stay sharp and be silent as possible. Our Murderer might still be here." Just then, he said to one of the officer, "Lend me your gun" and so did the officer. Suddenly! "Wait, we three will go from here and you clowns go around so we bust the murderer from both sides." Jenkins,

Andrew and Roberto hid on the right of the wall, while the other two officers reached and hid on the left side of the wall. "On the count of 3...2...1, busted!" shouted Andrew turning around to the flashlight. And so did the other two officers. But there wasn't anyone alive there. Besides an on flashlight, there was a body of a women lying. And beside the body there was a metal can to which Andrew was just about to kick because of his frustration, when! "Don't!" Jenkins shouted. He went towards the can, picked it up and put it towards his nose. "Fascinating very, very fascinating." He said. "What do you mean" Andrew questioned. "I know you've found something Leigh, now spit it out." Said Robeerto. "Alright listen carefully" said Jenkins. He started. "So back near the stairs, I sensed some ugly smell; well the officers said that one went to smoke while the other went to grab a short drink to the car. But the first one`s mouth wasn't smelling neither the second one had an empty bottle. So were they lying? No they weren't. You see this cylinder; this has some gaseous hallucinogen, so these guys weren't lying. They were just drugged and the murderer was present here until I and Andrew arrived. So when the murderer drugged them both, he started dragging the woman. But why would he drag her, instead of just picking her? It's simple our murderer is disabled." said

Jenkins. "What about the flash light then?" asked Andrew. "I don't know" said Jenkins. "He`ll solve that too" said Robeerto. "Let's inspect the body, shall we?" Andrew asked. "Of course" said Jenkins. Both of them went towards the body to turn it over, as it was lying on the stomach. They turned it over. And then! Jenkins was in horror."Alright, you take the picture of the face; we need to identify the body." Robeerto said to one of the officer. "I....I ....don't think that would be necessary" said Jenkins. "You know her" Andrew asked "Name: Annie Skarts. Age: twenty five" Jenkins said tearfully. He stood up and a stream of tears came out of his eyes. And at the moment he fell on his knees. Looking downwards to the ground and his hair covering half his face. Roberto came near him and put a helping hand on his shoulder. "Leigh, it's alright son. It's alright." He said. "No offense old man. I don't need your condolence. I am fine." He stood up and his head straight forward. "So guys, you see this blood line, below the gut, I think she was stabbed." Said Andrew. "I have seen the body Roberto, cover her." Jenkins said. "Wait we have to take a photograph" said Andrew. "I said cover it you..." Jenkins shouted and caught his collar. "Leigh! Wait son." Said Robeerto. Jenkins stopped at the moment and he let go. "First we deal with the scene" said Jenkins. Roberto asked the two officers to cover the body, while Andrew called the police ambulance. The ambulance came within minutes, and they went up to the road. Placed the body in the ambulance. "Hey, grey head, you have water?" asked Jenkins. "I have" Said Roberto. He reached the pocket inside his overcoat, and removed a small bottle, handed it to Jenkins. "Thanks, grey head" said Jenkins. Then Jenkins took a sip and he started. "So our murderer was here till you brats arrived, not you grey head. Then when these two punks were standing near Annie, the murderer released the hallucionogen, it might have been really strong, and such strong hallucinogen isn't available in drug markets." Jenkins said. "Hospital or highly qualified chemists." Said Andrew. "Correct" said Jenkins. Then he continued. "So when we were following the drag trail, I saw a light flicker, that time the murderer was hiding there and was trying to throw Annie in the river. And when he saw us coming, he abandoned the idea of disposing and ran for his life. Another thing, our murderer is disabled. Because if he was an average sized or normal, then he could have picked Annie`s corpse, instead of dragging her all the way there. Hey you punks I want all the area photographed and yes, Robeerto I have to inform Ben. You have a phone?" Asked Jenkins. "Yes there is one in the car" Said Robeerto. "Alright" said Jenkins, and he moved towards the old man`s car. He took a phone and dialled to Benjamin Steel. After a few rings, Ben picked up. "Hello, this is Benjamin Steel, may I know who has called?" his voice seemed a bit sad."Ben, this is Leigh. I am afraid I have terrible news, Ben" said Jenkins. "Wait, Leigh, I know the news. I will make it easy for you. I, killed Annie! And yes I want to surrender. I am going to yard`s police station. Farewell, Leigh." Said Ben. Something about his tone was not correct. "Ben, you are not going anywhere, I am coming there Understand? I am coming there myself." Said Jenkins. "Okay, Leigh." Said Ben and hung up the phone. Without wasting any time Jenkins rushed to Robeerto. "Oldie, there is a problem. I need to go to Ben`s as soon as possible." Said Jenkins. "Alright, what do we do of Annie?" asked Robeerto. "Look, I trust very limited people in this city, do not go to any yard based Forensic Laboratory. Go to Dr.Petro Blue. He is one we can trust. And listen I'll take Andrew with me." Said Jenkins. He ordered Andrew and both started running towards the nearest Bus stop, when Robeerto shouted. "Leigh, go take my car" he handed Jenkins the keys and said. "You have saved my ass, many a times, Leigh. Don't worry I`ve got your back." He said. "Thanks Grey head" said Jenkins. They sat in the car and started straight towards Ben`s house. "Hey, Leigh, I mean sir." Said

Andrew. "No, don't call me `sir` Leigh or Jenkins is fine. Jenkins declared. "Okay Leigh, well I am sorry for there. I didn't know she, was your best friend." Said Andrew. "She is and will always be my best friend. Not a problem, and I was the one who lost my temper that time, so I am sorry." Said Jenkins. "Its fine, well who is Ben?" asked Andrew. "Her fiancée" said Jenkins. "And he killed her?" asked Andrew. "Honestly, I don't think so." Jenkins answered. "And why do you think so?" Andrew asked. "Gut feeling!" said Jenkins. "Since when did `The` Leigh Jenkins start to believe in gut feelings?" Andrew asked again. "Look, novice there are a lot of things you don't know." Said Jenkins. "Then tell me."Andrew said. "Alright. Here" Jenkins started. "Ben was a fine man since his child hood. A smart one. Annie liked him since then. But he was a bit confused. One hell of a person he is. A few years ago, he lost Karla, his elder sister and her fiancée in a car crash. And guess what, Ben made the car himself. So he blamed himself for their deaths. He was broken after that. Until Annie proposed him for marriage." Jenkins Narrated. "I can understand the man`s total pain. He is relatable." Said Andrew. "I know" said Jenkins. "I am kind of excited to meet him" Andrew declared. "We'll see" said Jenkins.

After a couple of minutes they reached Ben`s house. They rang the bell, and waited for a couple of minutes. But no one answered. Then Jenkins rang the bell several times and knocked, when he noticed, that the door was locked from outside. "Why did he leave when I told him to stay?" Said Jenkins agitatedly. "you got a phone?" he asked to Andrew. "Yes" Andrew answered. Jenkins took the phone and called his friend in the nearest police station. "Hey frost, this is Leigh. Tell me is Ben present there?" asked Jenkins and waited for his reply. "Alright, thanks frost." He hung up and said "He isn't there." "Then where is he?" asked Andrew. "Only one way to find out. Out of my way, novice." Said Jenkins. He ran towards the door and kicked it hard. "We could have used a master key" said Andrew. They went inside. "Go check upstairs, I'll check here." Jenkins first went from the passage to the living room, where he found nothing. Then he was going towards the dining room, when he sensed a familiar smell. He was just about to enter the dining room when he cut a string that was attached in such way that if hampered it would release the lock of two metallic cylinders attached on the inside edges of the entrance to the dine. Jenkins cut the string unknowingly and as soon as he entered two clouds of white smoke pounced on his face. He closed his eyes in reflex and started coughing. The gas was so strong that Jenkins couldn't resist. Somehow he managed to come out of the range of the gas towards the dine. He opened his eyes and saw. "Annie!" he could not believe what he was seeing. He saw a younger version of himself, Annie and Ben on the little Brink. "Go on Leigh you were going to tell us the story of the five pigs." Said Annie. "Ann, it's called `Five little pigs` and is written by Agatha Christie. The finest Crime story writer." Said Ben "And it has my favourite detective, Hercule Poirot." Leigh. "Hey guys, so what do you want to become when you grow up six inches tall?" Asked Ben. "I want to be an actress just like Olivia Newton." Annie said. "What about you Leigh."Ben asked. "Oh, I know he wants to become Hercule Poirot, when he grows" said Annie. "Not just Hercule Poirot, I want to become Shercule Poiromes" Said Leigh. "And what about you Ben?" Annie asked "I want to be a racer just like Ken Miles. And when I will win Le Mans, you both will be in the audience VIP section. And when I`ll come there with the winner`s bouquet and three or four girls with me, you both will come towards me and then we will party together." Said Ben. Annie made a jealous face and said "Only if we stay together till we grow up" then Leigh, said "Annie, Ben I am here because of you both. I promise you guys, we will always be together. And if anything wrong happens with us, I will be there to save us like Robin Hood. Because I will be...." Annie cut Leigh and said "Yes, Shercule Poiromes." Suddenly everything blacked out in front of Jenkins, who was seeing himself as child. And an adult version of Annie appeared. "Annie!" Jenkins said with a subtle smile. But something about her was weird. She gave an evil smile and said "You failed us, you failed us." She seemed hurt and then tears started to come out of her eyes. Jenkins was also tearful at the moment "Annie, we are together, we, please Ann, don't cry please." He said. "You failed us, Leigh, you failed us." She said again. "Jenkins! Jenkins!" a voice came from behind the smoke. Jenkins fell on his knees saying "Why did it have to be you, Ann, Why?" he shouted. Just then Andrew emerged out of the smoke and saw him on his knees, helpless. "Andrew saw something very disturbing on the dining table. And Jenkins fainted. "Oh, no, no, no, not now Jenkins" said Andrew.

"Wake up" "wake up Leigh." "Jenkins." Jenkins heard two to three voices. He opened his eyes. Then he coughed. "What, what happened at Ben`s house. Wait where are we?" Jenkins asked. "We are at" said Andrew when Jenkins said cutting him off "Petro's laboratory, I figured that." Said Jenkins. "Well, what happened at Ben's house,

Andrew where is he?" Jenkins asked. "We got a bad news J" Said Petro Blues. "What?" Jenkins asked again. "When we reached Ben's house we thought that he went to the police station, but you called at the top station and he wasn't there. We broke in the house. You told me to go upstairs. You were checking down, when you went in the kitchen, you accidently cut the string that unleashed the hallucinogen gas cylinders on the edges. I came down after calling you multiple times. You did not answer, so I came down. I saw the smoke; you were on your knees. When I came there you fainted." Andrew stated. "We don't have good news, Leigh." Said Robeerto. "Tell me whatever it is." Declared Jenkins. "Ben's gone Leigh, we found, Andrew found him dead." Robeerto Declared. Jenkins had the same expression as before. His head was down, his hair covering half his face. "Anything, else!" He asked. His tone was so dull he was almost broken. It was like someone sucked out his soul from his body. At the moment he seemed like living dead. "Here" said Andrew while handing him a piece of paper covered in a plastic packet. It was note. Jenkins began to read.

Leigh

I won't say I am sorry to do this to you. How broken you will be after reading this I know. But still I can't accept the fact that I have taken two most precious lives to me. Well Karla and Spencer were driving the car that I made them. And the report said that brakes failed at the sudden. So I guess I killed both of them. Leigh, yes they died because of me. I did not make it clear earlier, but I did not kill both of them for Karla's money and estate. I think you are the only person who can understand me now. I know you told me to stay at my home, I stayed. There is one more thing I want to tell you, brother. From last three weeks I am having a mental break down, and I am seeing a psychiatrist. Yes. I directly wanted to come to you, but I didn't. I am seeing visions, leigh. Visions, of spencer and Karla. He is alive. And last thing of all. I killed Annie.

Yours truly

Benjamin Steel.

Tears started coming from his eyes as he finished reading. "What a bloody liar." Shouted Jenkins. "He did not kill her, he did not kill her!" Jenkins shouted. "But this is what he said" said Petro. "No, no, no, you guys don't know him as I know. He is a man that can't even kill an ant" Jenkins Declared. "Then why did he say so?" Petro Asked "It might be something else, wait petro did you conduct the autopsy?" Jenkins asked. "Yes you were sleeping for quite a time so I could conduct both autopsies" Said Petro. "Then tell me what you got" said Jenkins. "Alright, so we'l start from Annie. She was shot in the thigh which disabled her from walking. Then she was strangled to death." Said Petro. 'Beware you homicidal Brat, because I am going to kill you the same way you killed Annie, just you see.' Thought Jenkins. "And about Ben, when Mr. Bridge found him, there was a revolver in his right hand and the bullet crossed his head from right side, so I guess, he killed himself." Petro said. "Could be." Said Jenkins. Petro came towards Jenkins and said, "There is one more thing, common between you three guys, there was a concentrated amount of LSD in all of your bloods. Well I took a sample of yours when you were asleep." Said Petro. "Yes, I figured when I woke" Declared Jenkins. "Okay that's it." said Petro. "What else we've got from Ben's house?" Jenkins asked to Andrew. "Well a couple of pharmaceutical prescriptions, the revolver, the suicide note, yeah that's it" said Andrew. "Okay, Petro take charge of the prescriptions, you show me the revolver" said Jenkins. Andrew handed him the gun. "Colt .45 1878 vintage" said Andrew. "Brilliant" said Jenkins. Then Jenkins removed the revolver from the plastic bag. "Don't tamper it" said Andrew. "Shut it novice I know what I am doing." Jenkins declared. He turned the gun around to check its Butt. There was something inscribed on the dorsal side of the butt. `To, my brother Spencer Alter` "Wait I have seen this gun earlier" said Jenkins. "Where?" asked Andrew. "This is the gun that Ben bought to gift it to Spencer, his would be Brother in law." Jenkins declared. "Petro, tell me you did not dispose the bullet from Annie`s thigh and Ben`s head?" said Jenkins. "Yes, I did not." Petro stated. "You are learning from your past mistakes. Good to know that" said Jenkins. "Yes, I am trying to be more conscious, because the last time I wasn't, it cost me an important life." Said petro. "Show me the bullets" Jenkins ordered. "Here" said Petro, handing him a watch glass with two red coloured bullets. Jenkins took a microscope which was lying on the table, and then he observed both the bullets. "Both are of same size" he said. Then he took one bullet and went to a basin and washed it to see its colour. This was Black with yellow stripes. "Andrew, check the barrel, and give me one bullet from it" Jenkins ordered. Andrew checked the barrel. "Six shelled, only four bullets remaining."Andrew said. "Remove one bullet from the gun and show it to me" Jenkins ordered. So did Andrew. Jenkins then observed the third bullet. "Now this is not good." Said Jenkins. "All the three bullets are same, and the two were fired from the same gun." He said. "The gun is in possession of Ben that, that means, Ben really killed Annie." Said Andrew. "Do not say that, novice." Exclaimed Jenkins. "Whatever" said Andrew. "Cut it guys. I saw the prescriptions, and there is too much of psilocybin products in these." Said Petro. "What?" said Andrew in a sudden shock. "Why would a doctor suggest hallucinogen to a patient who is already having mental breakdown?" asked Andrew. "What is the name of the Doctor, Petro?" Jenkins asked. "It's signed as `Freddy Simpson, Victoria hospital." Said Petro. "Well I still have the question, why would a doctor prescribe hallucinogens to a patient who is having mental breakdowns." Andrew asked again. "Une facon de le savoir" said Jenkins. "Let's go then" said Robeerto who was excited seeing the young detective. "Be careful, you guys." Said Petro. Just then Jenkins noticed his overcoat lying on the floor. "que se passe-t-il, who did this" he exclaimed. "Uhhh, ummm" petro gave a grin. "This is not the way you treat clothes Petro. Jenkins said. "Okay, let's move" said Andrew. "After you" ordered Jenkins. Then Jenkins picked his trench coat flipped it in style and wore it. Andrew opened the door and started out. "Leigh!" said Robeerto. "What is it greyhead?" Jenkins asked. "We will cross any limits to find the killer. But tell me, are you ready to do what needs to be done." Robeerto said. First time in five years, Jenkins gave a sigh. "Je ne sais pas, what is bigger? Vengeance or justice, sometimes Vengeance is the appropriate justice" Jenkins quoted. "I know you won't fail my teaching leigh." Said Robeerto. "et si je dois?" said Jenkins. "We will see." Answered Robeerto. Then they started out and caught up with Andrew. "Has anyone got a cell phone? I need to call someone." Said Jenkins. Andrew handed him his cell phone. "You guys keep going towards the parking I will be behind." Said Jenkins and dialled a number. "Hey Gwen, its Leigh. Yeah, I am having a tough evening, hope at least you could sleep well? Ohh that's good. Well listen I am after something, I don't know how much time this will take, but I need to catch up with you after this is over. I really want to see you." Said Jenkins. Then he hung up. "C'mon guys lets go to Ben's house first, I think I need something from there." Said Jenkins. "Yes Boss" Said Andrew. "Since when did this guy start calling me 'Boss'" Jenkins said to Robeerto, by stressing on the word."Hey, Jenkins, you told me that you have a story right. After all this is over I hell want to hear it." said Andrew. "Alright Novice, I'll tell you all." Said Jenkins. "Well will you stop calling me that?" Said Andrew. "Oh, no not at all, novice" said Robeerto. "You too" said Andrew.

They arrived at Ben's house after an hour. "I will go alone. You guys wait here." Jenkins ordered. And he went inside. Without wasting much of time, he went directly to Ben's Bedroom. He opened the closet, and searched for a photo frame. A photo frame of him Ben and Annie. He pulled the frame and a chit fell down after it. Jenkins picked it and opened it. It said 'The blood of Karla Steel and Spencer Alter lies on your hand. You will pay with your life.' "Fascinating very, very fascinating" said Jenkins. He then went to the car. "Hey greyhead, keep this thing safe" Said Jenkins to Robeerto handing him the frame. "Yes Leigh." Said Robeerto.

They arrived at Victoria Hospital within an hour. They went to the reception. The table was covered with white sun mica and green stripes on it. On the other side of the table there was a lady with brown hair standing, Jenkins read the name plate on the table kept beside the computer. Beside the computer was a half-filled coffee cup. "Hope you are enjoying your coffee, Claire" Said Jenkins. Beside the woman there was a blonde haired man, sitting on the chair. "Oh, well yes, Mr...." said the woman, "Leigh Jenkins, pleased to meet you miss." Said Jenkins offering a handshake. The woman blushed and said "How may I help you Mr. Jenkins." She said. "Well,

Miss.Claire I am here to meet Dr. Freddy Simpson." Said Jenkins. When he said the name the man sitting beside Claire was shocked. And Andrew noticed his expression. He started staring at the man. "Amm, we don't have anyone named Freddy Simpson practicing here." Said Claire. Andrew came near Jenkins and whispered "That man beside her was shocked when you took the name." "Alright, thank you Miss Claire. We will just go." Said Jenkins. They went outside. "Hey Claire, I am not feeling well, I think I need to go home and take some rest." Said the man beside her. "Okay" Claire said. He took his bag and went out. He reached the parking. A punch fell on his face. He collapsed instantly. Andrew pulled him by his collar and then punched hard in his gut. He spitted blood. "Tell me what you know about Freddy Simpson." Asked Jenkins emerging from the shadows. "Like I am going to tell you mice" the man said. Andrew punched his right cheek resulting him falling down and a tooth came out of his mouth. Then Jenkins kicked hard on his gut, he spitted more blood. "I am not going to ask again" said Andrew by grabbing him by his collar. While Robeerto was standing behind seeing the torture. He removed a metal cased bottle and took a long sip from it. The voice of Robeerto gulping wine ,reached the three of them. Andrew took out his gun, and pointed towards the man.

"I am not going to ask again" Andrew declared. "Alright, alright." The man said.

"My name is Joseph" said the man. "Not interested in you" said Jenkins. "Okay, Freddy Simpson was not a doctor, indeed; he had a fake degree and a fake licence to practice. He is one legged man. His fake specialisation was in psychology. He came in this hospital. And I found out about his true nature. I blackmailed him that I'll tell everything to the yard. And I filled my pockets through him. But yes he may not be a doctor, but he knows how to use drugs very well." Said the man. "Where is he now?" Andrew asked. "Oh I don't know." Joseph answered. Jenkins punched hard on his face. Another of his tooth came out huddling. He coughed "Okay, okay, Building f, old Nichol street 11th floor flat 20." Said Joseph. "How do I know this is correct?" Andrew asked. While Jenkins directly stared in Joseph's eyes. "He is telling the truth." Declared Jenkins. "Then what are we waiting for?" Asked Robeerto. Andrew pushed Joseph down. "Let's go then" Said Andrew. The trio went to the car and started out. While the knelt Joseph took out his cell and dialled "They are coming for you, prepare it" Said Joseph and hung up.

After an hour they reached to the building. "Greyhead call one armed unit." Said Jenkins. "Okay" Robeerto said and went for his wireless in the car. "This is senior lieutenant Robeerto King'sman I need a unit of four at Building f, old Nichol Street. Over and out." Said Robeerto. "Alright, greyhead, you stay down at the entrance, Andrew and I will go up and bring the mouse down." Declared Jenkins. "I will, Leigh but promise me one thing; you will stick to what I taught you." Robeerto pleaded. Jenkins sighed. "I don't think I will." He said. "Let's go" Robeerto stood on the entrance while both of them started.

"Wait" Said Jenkins. "What?" asked Andrew. "You take the stairs, I will take the lift." Jenkins ordered. He went in the lift, Andrew took the stairs. Jenkins clicked the button written 11 on it. He closed his eyes and took a deep breath. 'Leigh, you are a good man. I know you will do what is needed.' Annie's voice popped in his mind. 'Leigh, I did it, I killed Ann' he heard Ben's voice. 'Promise me Leigh, you will stick to what I taught you.' Said Robeerto. Then he began to remember his childhood. His memories with Annie and Ben on the Brink. He took one deep breath again. And this time Gwen's face flashed in front of him. His good old memories were disturbed by a bell sound of the Elevator. Beyond the elevator lied Jenkins's true character. He took another breath. 'Let's do it' he thought and opened the door. Andrew was yet to come.

Jenkins saw a door with number plate '11' written on it. The door was half opened. He kicked it hard and went inside. He saw a hall. And all types of antique Arms were hanging on the walls. He noticed a black coat cloth hanging. He understood what it was. "It's over, Freddy Simpson. Or shall I say, Spencer Alter. A man wearing black overcoat and with a crutch came out. He was an average heighted black haired and blue eyed man. There were scar lines on his face. Something about him was peculiarly disgusting. Jenkins directly stared in his eyes. He saw there the hunger for vengeance. "You ugly little brat" said Jenkins and pounced on him.

They both collided resulting both of them falling out in the passage. Spencer fell towards the gate of the elevator while Jenkins fell near the stairs. Spencer struggled to stand and Jenkins did it in a second. Spencer removed a gun from his pocket and pointed it towards Jenkins. "Yeah, so you are going to kill me. Just try it." Said Jenkins. "Worse than that" Spencer answered while removing a can. And he sprayed it on Jenkins before he could react.

"You failed me Leigh, you failed us." Said Annie all this was going in front of Jenkins's eyes and Spencer was enjoying seeing him suffer. "You were my best friend and you failed me." Said Annie. Jenkins fell on his knees and said. "No, no Annie, I am sorry, I am sorry Annie." Said Jenkins , Spencer pointed his gun and said "First I make ye suffer, then send you to hell. He gave an evil smile and his finger was on the trigger. He was about to shoot. He pushed the trigger. And shot!

Before the bullet could touch Jenkins, Andrew pounced him pushing him out and stabbing a syringe in his neck. Jenkins was pushed aside but Andrew fell instantly. Jenkins came back to senses. Andrew wasn't able to stand up. Bullet had hit him below the heart. Seeing a chance Spencer went inside the elevator and clicked the lower ground button. There was some life left in Andrew. Jenkins pulled him gently, and rested his back against a pillar. "Go, he is getting away." He said. "I never leave my allies behind" Jenkins replied. "He will get away, there is a back door. Robeerto is unaware about it, go" Andrew said. Jenkins loosened his tie and tied it on Andrew's wound. "Just stay alive novice" Jenkins said and rushed down. He ran down till the fourth floor and the elevator was on the second. Jenkins saw a thick metal rod. He picked it and pushed it in the gate of fourth floor and opened the door. Resulting the elevator to stop on the second floor. Spencer somehow managed to open the door with his crutch, and came out. He started huddling down the floor when Jenkins pounced on him. They both fell on the stairs and started rolling down. Both of them came on the ground floor. Spencer's crutch fell down. But he aimed his gun on Jenkins's head. Jenkins stared directly in his eyes. His gun fell he managed to pick his crutch and run. Jenkins started walking in an evil manner towards him. After a distance, Spencer removed a small metal can. He was about to spray when!

Robeerto King's man hit Spencer's head hard with his walking stick. He fell on his knee instantly. A stream of blood started to come from back of his ear. A huge smile struck on Robeerto's face. "I get to save your ass, once in my life." The old man said. "Quick go upstairs. Andrew is hit." Jenkins said. Robeerto rushed up.

"Now, it's you and me." Jenkins said. "Tell me, why?" Jenkins asked. "Ha ha ha. I don't need to confess Mr. Jenkins. You are clever enough." Said Spencer. Jenkins picked him by the collar and threw him down. Then he picked the gun and shot his thigh. "Aaghhh!" Spencer shouted painfully. "Go on, strangle me. Just like I killed your friend. What was her name? Aah! Annie, of course." Said Spencer. "You dare say her name!" Jenkins shouted and then started to strangle him. He pushed too hard. Just then, both of his friend`s faces flashed in his mind.

Gwen's smiling face struck him. He loosened his grip. Then he slapped him hard. Spencer fainted; just then two officers came walking towards them. "We will take good care of him sir." One of them said. "Cuff him, and take out gas cans from him if you find any." Jenkins ordered and rushed upwards.

Andrew was lying on the ground, his back resting on the elevator door. "Le...Leigh" Andrew said. "I am here Andrew." Jenkins said softly. "I...If you f...Ind my sister, Leigh. Tell her. Tell her I miss her." Andrew handed him a photo stained with blood. "Jule" he said with whatever remaining strength he had. His vision started blurring. He exhaled his last berth. Jenkins closed Andrew's eyes with his palm. Robeerto was tearful "One hot blood, he was." Jenkins kept his hand on Robeerto's shoulder. "I remember what you taught me, Robeerto."Said Jenkins. He glanced at the photo. There was a little blonde haired boy and a ginger haired girl. "She resembles little Annie doesn't she?" Asked Jenkins. "Yeah" said Robeerto. "You goanna be okay old man?" Jenkins Asked."Yes I think I will" Said Robeerto.

Spencer was then handcuffed and kept in the police car. An ambulance arrived some minutes later, to take Andrew's corpse. "So now what are you going to do

Robeerto?" Jenkins Asked."I will go to the Colonel Fawcett and grab a drink. You care to join?" Robeerto asked to Jenkins. "Thanks for asking, but I got a job to do." Declared Jenkins by looking at the photo Andrew gave him. "Right then, tell me if you need anything Leigh. I will be there for you." Robeerto Said. "Thanks, Grey head." Jenkins said and they dispersed.

Five Months Later. Little port, King Shore Drive, London.

"Tell me why you called me here Grey head" Jenkins Asked. "I wanted to tell you something." Robeerto said. "But why here?" Jenkins asked. "I wanted to make sure that the thing which started here ends here itself." Said Robeerto. "Good thought." Said Jenkins "I made sure he is hanged." Robeerto Declared. Now tell me everything from the start." Said Robeerto. "Soon Gwen will be here Robeerto." Said Jenkins. "It won't take time, just five minutes." Robeerto pleaded. "Okay listen then" Jenkins said. "The story starts seven years from now. At this place. In 1996, there was a car crash. A woman called Klara Steel, which happens to be Ben's sister and her fiancé Spencer Alter were driving a car at high speed. Then suddenly the brakes fail. There was nothing Spencer could do. The car crashed, and Klara died instantly. We thought that Spencer died with her. But no, he just lost one leg in that fatal crash. The car was designed and engineered by Ben. So Ben thought he indirectly killed both of them. In these years, Spencer made a plan to take revenge. He learned all about chemicals and hallucinogens that he could. To get revenge he targeted Annie. He started to drug her mysteriously; yes I got a solution for that. Annie used to do mental checkups every month in the Victoria hospital. She was a mentally strong woman but still she believed in Regular checkups. When Dr. Freddy Simpson started to do her checkups, he said she had some neural problems and prescribed concentrated dose of Hallucinogens to her. She started to have mental breakdowns. At the evening of the murder when I was in the museum, she was given one concentrated dose. She thought that Ben called her at the brink. But no. Dr. Freddy Simpson or shall I say Spencer Alter called her there. She was surprised to see him there he shot her thigh causing her unable to walk then he sprayed the instant hallucinogen gas on her so she hallucinates and he can kill her with an ease. He was going to dispose her body off, when an old man saw her body and reported. He was hiding near the pillar, till you guys arrived. When Andrew came to call me, he somehow managed to drug the two guards and dragged her body towards the river.

But he abandoned the idea when he saw us coming towards the pillar. He left his flash light there in a hurry.

From there he went straight to Ben's. He knew I would be going there. He then drugged Ben and made him kill himself, with the gun he shot Annie, so we think that Ben was the one who killed her. Then he set the hallucinogen trap for me. I knew that there might be more traps like this in his house, and especially for me. So I told Petro to prepare drug buster. He could only prepare one; he did not have enough material. I gave that syringe to Andrew so at the time he could inject me. Which he did indeed. Then we caught him. Game over." Jenkins concluded. "I want to ask something, you know the whole story, then why ask me again?" He said. "I wanted to know about the gun and all that exactly happened." Robeerto answered. "And congratulations Leigh, you played Sherlock again" he said. "Next time Sir, I will try to play Leigh Jenkins" He said. "I was kidding" Robeerto said. "Well" said Jenkins. Robeerto left.

Gwen arrived after some time. Both of them sat on a bench. "I don't know Gwen, am I ever going to heal from this, and what I did back there, sparing his life. Was that any good?" Said Jenkins. "We know that he would have been killed any way, don't worry Leigh, you let vengeance fall and Justice rise. You did the right thing. You did not kill him. That makes you different from him. Justice was the right scythe for him. Gwen said. She rested her head on his shoulder. Together they gazed the beautiful sunset.

Chapter 3

On Trail of Vengeance.

"You mess with me, I kick your ass." Said a bald man, punching Leigh on face. As for London`s best private detective Leigh Charles Jenkins, he had found himself tied on a wooden chair in the crime lord Hercules Bolzano's temporary hideout. "Where are the damn diamonds, you sloppy piece of shit" said the crime lord. *"Dans ton putain d`estomac"* said Jenkins "Who the hell taught you French?" the crime lord asked. "Votre fille Amanda" Jenkins answered with a smile. The crime lord punched him with his right hand, which was equipped with brass knuckles and said "meurs toi chien" a blot of blood ran out of Leigh`s mouth. When suddenly a phone kept on the near table started ringing. Bolzano looked at it, he was annoyed. He went towards it and picked it up. *"va te faire foutre"* said the crime lord and was about to hang up the phone when, Leigh pounced on him instantly untying his wrist and legs. He punched the criminal on the face. The mobile went flying in the air, two guards near the door armed with knives charged straight towards him. Leigh caught the phone and put it on his ear while tackling the men with knives. "Detective Jenkins here" he said on the phone. While the crime lord removed his gun and pointed towards him. "You are so dead" said the crime lord. "In middle of something" he said. The crime lord gave an amused look. "Work it silently bald boy I am talking to a client. Ohh not to you sweet lady." Said Jenkins. While Bolzano pressed the trigger, there was a click sound and nothing happened. Jenkins gave a smile and put his hand in the pocket of his trench coat and removed a bullet magazine ,threw it out of the glass window. Then he started running up a staircase evading every goon that came in the way and simultaneously talking with a woman on his phone. Soon reached on the top of the building, which was adjacent to the river. While Bolzano and the other thugs chased him. Jenkins climbed the railing. "Nowhere to hide Piggy" said Bolzano "*au revoir meunier*" said Jenkins giving a two finger salute and jumped on his back. Bolzano sighed and said, "I wanted to kill him myself" "Boss he is not dead" said a goon. Bolzano stared down from the railing. Jenkins was lying smiling on a garbage boat.

"Alright, tell me the name again. " Jenkins asked on the phone. "Tom Frank" said the girl on the phone. "Alright I'll be there, but my ticket and stay is your responsibility." Said Jenkins "Alright" said the girl on the phone. "See you Miss..." Jenkins took a pause. "Captain Riana Brooks" said the woman. "Yes, see you ma`am" said Jenkins and hung up. 'What a pleasant place for me to get a nap' Jenkins said to himself. After seeing his surroundings he said "Can't even get a good night sleep can I"

"Is this guy dead?" said a janitor. "No he is asleep" said another "I recognize him, he is the detective." Said the first. "How do we wake him up" said the second one. "I am pretty sure he's dead. Said the first one. Just then Leigh opened his eyes and yawned. He saw both of them and said "Ohh, good evening gentlemen. I am here already, how fast. "You are at Martin`s" Jenkins cut him and said "Martins Dump yard I know. My house is eight miles from this messy place." "Alright sir, all the best." Said the first janitor awkwardly. "Ohh wa...wait I need some money for a cab." Said Jenkins. "Why would we give you money?" asked one of the janitors. "Oh yes right you are the labors. Anyway can you call Martin for me?

Tell him his old friend is here to see him." Jenkins said. "Whatever." Said the janitor. He went towards a cabin. "Hey boss, there is a freak outside, who says that he is your old friend." the janitor said to Martin. Who removed his cigarette and dusted it on the dirty ashtray. "Okay I am coming." Said Martin. He then came out and saw Jenkins. "Who are you? I don't know you." Said Martin. "Oh Martin don't you recognize me. I am Leigh, your old budd." Jenkins said. "Hey you two, I think this is a drunkard. Throw him outta here." Martin ordered to both the janitors. "Oh wait no, I just want fifteen pounds." Jenkins demanded. "Alright now beat him up and then throw him out." Martin ordered. "Okay Martin, I am going out but I won't tell anyone that you actually kidnapped your own daughter to take money from your own wife and then you spent it all in poker, then you broke in John Doe`s house, one of the most reputed detective in Scotland yard and stole the blue prints of Scotland Yard HQ and sold it to a man wearing a black coat yesterday night." Jenkins said. Martin`s jaw was wide open. "Wa...Wait, here is twenty pounds." Said Martin, handing him the money. "And how do you know all that?" he asked. "Oh well, your locket, there is a girl with you and a woman. By judging the photo is bit torn, and small corrosion stains, I can say that the locket is at least ten years old, well and the girl is new born so that means she is ten now. And the question of you kidnapping your own daughter is because you have no guts to kidnap someone other`s child. If I am not wrong you kidnapped her because you wanted to extort money from your wife who took your own money which you got as a bonus. So the money you extorted from your wife was spent in poker, yesterday you went at a cheap bookie's where you lost it all, I can see that from that compensation batch on your shirt, generally cheap bookies give such things to losers when they lose it all, basically to advertise their business, seriously you didn't take a bath today. Then the blue prints, yesterday evening Detective Doe`s locker was broken and some thing important  was stolen,the burglar was caught in camera while breaking his window, where he got a wound on his right arm, oh well is that the arm where you have a bandage , he was 5`5 so are you." Jenkins stopped and took a breath. "Man, anyway I have given you extra five pounds to zip your mouth, and you are going to do that exactly." Said Martin. "I will think about it." Jenkins Declared. "Hey you, you are going to shut your mouth" said Martin. Jenkins coughed sarcastically. "You are not going to tell anyone." Martin repeated still a bit of anger. Jenkins coughed again.

"Please sir. Do not tell anyone." Said Martin politely. "Better" declared Jenkins. Then he left.

Half an hour later, Jenkins arrived at his house in Paddington. He rolled in the flat where his land lady Mrs. Jonas was waiting for him. "There you are Leigh, where were you" she asked. "Well let's say I was almost killed by French Mafia. "What!" exclaimed Mrs. Jonas "Oh relax Mrs. J you think that, a couple of puny Mafia can kill me" he said. "Oh dear, what would Gwen think if she comes to know." said Mrs. Jonas. "Its not a big deal Mrs. J. But if I tell her that I am bringing her a Christian Bale autograph, then?" Said Jenkins. "Wait, is he is in London. Why is he in London, he lives in LA.?" Mrs. Jonas said. "Yes he lives in LA" Jenkins declared. "Oh dear so he is here, where is he" Said Mrs. Jonas excitedly. "N…no, no Mrs. Jonas." He said. "Wait does that mean you, oh dear you are going to LA." She asked rushing towards him. "Happy realization Mrs. Joanne Jonas." He said. "Oh dear why do you stink Leigh. Were you sleeping in garbage?" she asked. "Oh you are precisely correct." He declared. "Oh, Mrs. J, I am short of time my flight is at 9 sharp. Let me pack I have to leave." He cried. "Now Leigh Charles Jenkins, you are not going to leave this house without taking a shower, and if you would then you will have to go over my dead body." She shouted. "Where is the revolver?" he asked "Oh, I was really kidding dear." She declared. "So was I" he said, kissed her on the cheek, removed his trench coat and rushed to the bathroom. She went to the telephone and called Gwen

Leigh boarded the US government private jet sharp at nine and the plane took off. 'The best time to do what I have not done in ages, get a good night sleep.' He thought and went to sleep.

Eleven and a half an hour later the detective found himself at LAX airport. Where he saw two cop cars waiting for him. He just walked towards them with his luggage, when a Lady with short afro curls, wearing a typical cop captain Uniform stepped out. The woman came near and offered a hand shake "Major Crimes Captain Arianna Bolt" she introduced. Leigh took the handshake and said "Private Detective Leigh Jenkins." He said. "Hop in Mr. Detective, you will be provided with the victim`s current report and background in the car. We will now go to the Major Crimes office; there I will introduce you to a couple of people with whom you will be working closely on this case. We will make his murder and your arrival official tomorrow. The fans are going to burn" she said. "Alright" he said and sat in the car. There a really expressionless cop handed him a file, he opened it and there was everything about Tom Frank`s murder and his life before it was printed in words and some photos were attached. Jenkins hardly read anything, he glanced all the photos. Then his attention was drawn to the neon light boards and huge buildings on the road. "Impressive." He said. "You will be even happier when you go inside one." The expressionless cop said. "So Mr. Jenkins I think that you might require to interrogate some of the celebs, so please be calm then, and do not do anything that a common man would do. Is that understood?" The captain said. "Yes ma`am." Jenkins answered.

Suddenly! The car Dashed on a building`s edge. "Oh crap and they call you the best cop car driver." The Captain yelled at the driver. The captain, Leigh and one officer stepped out of the car, Leigh went towards the back left wheel of the car, the tire was punctured. "Hey, your tire is gone out." He said to the officer. "I am so sorry ma`am, I`ll replace the tire." The officer said. He went to the trunk and removed a tire, harness and a jack. While, Jenkins was staring at the dark alley of the building. "Scared of dark allies?" The captain asked.

Jenkins was in his own state of haunt. A memory flashed in his mind `Run, run Leigh. Don't look back. ` A woman was shouting. Leigh was running through the alley when a man carrying a chainsaw with some amount of blood on it came right in front of him. `No where to hide in the darkness, you little shit.` Said the man with that chain saw.

"Hey? Hey Jenkins? Are you there?" the captain asked. Leigh jumped out of his good old memory. "Oh, what, yes... I am here, well does anyone have water?" he asked. "There is a bottle in the car" said the captain. He went towards the car and the driver handed him the bottle. He drank some and kept it back. He came back to the tire. Suddenly there was a sound of gunshot and everyone glanced towards the alley, while captain Bolt looked at her wrist watch. Three men armed with revolvers stepped out of the darkness. "Heya copies, throw down all your weapons." One of them ordered. "Now If I was to be a little hired struggling actor, then I wouldn't throw such attitude to real time Hollywood cops." Jenkins said giving a sarcastic look to the captain. All the gunmen sighed. "Alright go, get outta here, you are done." The captain ordered to three of them. "So how much did I score?" Leigh asked to the captain. "To be honest, 4 out of 5." Captain Bolt said. "Wait, why not 5 out of 5?" Jenkins asked. "You see Hollywood cops require an elaborated answer." She said. "Right then, let's start." Jenkins announced "Show me what have you got detective." She said. "So, before the tire got punctured, the driver was driving a bit slowly, as far as I think, you people don't drive that slow so the driver knew that the tire was going to puncture, and was driving slow for precaution. The tire did puncture, on the exact spot where you wanted it to be punctured, there was a pattern of holes on the tire, the pattern on the chains which you people use to puncture tires of criminal drivers. But cap, your plan did not go well as you wanted, you wanted the car to stop right in front of that dark alley. But it stopped a foot earlier. Thanks to the slow speed of the car. Then the three henchmen of yours, you expected them to come out as soon as the car stopped in front of the alley. When they came out you looked at your watch with dissatisfaction. The question of how I came to know they were fake is, here let me answer, first I know the sound of a real gun shot. The second, when you looked at the watch it became clear that you were not satisfied of something. What was that, we won't reach the office on time or something else? You told them to come out as soon as the car stops, so you were disappointed. The most important question of all, why did you set up this whole thing? Amm I have this answer too. I am a private detective so you wanted to check that is your case of the great Actor Tom Franks is in correct hands or not. Well let me tell you cap, I might be a private and not well trained like you, but there are many things that can be done more efficiently without being tied to the system, a system that blindly shakes hand with demons." Jenkins said giving a sigh of dissatisfaction. "Well, the result is now 6 out of 5, and Mr. Jenkins I clearly underestimated you." Said the Captain. The detective gave a slight smile.

They reached the Los Angeles Major Crimes department office. It was a quite busy place; most wanteds on the soft board, paperwork, piled up papers, two coffee tables, people chit chatting, officers and detectives working on computers, officers taking statements and some of them taking handcuffed people. Captain Bolt came in the center with Leigh. "Officers and detectives, I think you are familiar with the world class Detective, here I give You Leigh Jenkins. Take over Jenkins." She announced."Good evening ladies and gentlemen, I am private detective Leigh Jenkins. So I have travelled a lot for cases. But this is my first time in Hollywood. Now, first I must tell you that, no one here shall call me *Jenkins*, *Mr. Jenkins* or *Jen*. You people call me by my name and that's Leigh. "He said. "Alright, in my office." The captain said to Jenkins.

"So Leigh, you are assigned to solve the murder of Tom Franks. The L.A.P.D will help you as much as it can. You can keep your revolver in my office, you will be provided by an L.A.P.D issued gun, for defense you will only use that when required, and you are to rest in Jimmy Marshall's till the case is not solved, here is your pass for the lodge, and here is something special" she gave him the lodge pass and handed him a L.A.P.D senior detective badge. "Thanks captain, I am honored." Said Jenkins. A short ginger haired woman entered the office. "Samuleen Hawkins, reporting ma`am." The girl said. "Oh right, and Leigh, you will be helped by Hawkins on the case. Since London gave us their best, we give our best to help you." Said Bolt. "Pleasure to meet you Mr. Jenkins. My name is Samuleen Hawkins, you can call me Sam." The girl said offering a shake hand. Jenkins shook hands and said. "Pleasure mine, Sam and you may call me Leigh." "So how are you holding up in Hollywood?" she asked " well now I am in love with Hollywood." He said with a slight smile. She smiled too. "Ahem!" The captain coughed sarcastically.

"So now how do we start?" Jenkins asked. "Well, I think you are going to stay here for a while, so let's start from getting to know some famous people that might help in the investigation." Said Sam. "And how do we do that?" Jenkins asked. "Simple, I take you to a charity party." She said. "One of your friend died and you are hosting a party." Said Jenkins. "My friend Ryan is hosting a party tomorrow at his penthouse, It`s actually a fundraiser for The Director`s Guild so we can't actually call it off. I`ll be glad if you come...It...It would be important for the investigation." She said. "Wait...By Ryan, do you mean Ryan Johnson's?"  Jenkins asked. "I totally mean Ryan Johnson's. Sam said. "Alright, I`ll...I`ll come to the party with you.  But enough chit chat, so Sam can you revise Tom Frank`s murder?" Jenkins asked. "With pleasure, Two days before on December 1, evening 6.0`clock, Tom`s body was found in his Jacuzzi, there were no wounds on the body, he wasn't even strangled, forensics say that his heart just stopped. Surveillance footage was found in which a masked man that just broke in his house, was talking and threatening him. He removed his mask and Tom was shocked. He fell in the Jacuzzi. Then the recording was disturbed. To be personal, there was a phone call in Captain Bolt`s office. The guy who called said that he was going to kill Tom, he identified himself as *Hood*. A card was found by Tom`s body saying `*Your souls will keep wandering between heaven and hell*. So all we need to do is prove that this guy calling himself as

The hood killed Tom and hunt him down." Said Sam. "Oh boy, I just love mask murderers. So now let`s hunt the Hood." Said Leigh.

"I guess I can't come to the party Sam." Leigh said."Hey, why not?" she asked. "I really wanted to come but I don't have a proper outfit for that, besides who knew I would be invited to a Hollywood party." Said Jenkins. "It's alright Leigh; I know a place where you can buy a really nice Tux." Said Sam. "Oh, you really don't have to d-" before Jenkins could say something Sam interrupted. "Oh cut it Leigh, let me show you some Hollywood courtesy." She said. "Alright...alright you win" said Jenkins. "Okay meet me downstairs in ten minutes I just have a work to finish." She said and disappeared.

Ten minutes later Jenkins found himself sitting beside Sam in a car, they rushed towards the town. "Good guy, Tom was. A great friend of Ryan and Bruce. I think we all will miss him." She said in grief. "Any friend of Bruce and Ryan is a friend of mine." Said Sam. "Well, you seem to know quite about Ryan...And Bruce of course, and by Bruce you-" She cut him off and said. "Yes I do mean `the` Bruce Wilson." Sam declared. "I have heard these names quite a lot of times, Bruce Wilson, Ryan Johnson's I have seen Bruce`s work in many films like *The Cult, Olivia,*

Lands and Seas." Said Jenkins. "Oh he is super handsome, he is really sweet. Actually I know him for more than ten years; we and Ryan were in the same high school. Ryan and Bruce were... are the best of friends. So after high school they both went to acting school and I started my training." Said Sam. "I`ve seen Bruce`s comedy role in *Olivia,* indeed he did it with perfection, but there was a subtle, solemn pain in his eyes." Said Jenkins. "Look he is really a very nice person, and he tries to be nice with everybody. He is quite the tragedy, his parents died in a car crash a few years ago, and then he started to live with his grandfather when he was recently killed in a plane crash, the one that happened in Spain." Said Sam. "I am sorry, yes the one that crashed mysteriously?" Jenkins asked. "Yeah." She said. "Good gracious! How does he manage to look so jolly and productive all the time." He asked. "Well, Leigh I think I should ask you the same question. Captain Holt told me that you were a bit scared of that dark alley?" she asked. "Alright detective, you caught me. I completely disagree on the fact that time and situations mould us and make us who we are, there are no wrong choices made Sam, there were never. We have the capability of thinking and estimating the results of all choices we make and in every situation. We tend to make easy choices every time because we are too lazy to estimate their outcomes. It's not the situations that moulds us and makes us what we are. But what does is the efficiency of our mind to think a moralful way. A criminal is no one but a person in dilemma of choices, they act whatever seems easier, and they ignore looking towards the outcome out of laziness." Said Jenkins. "My god! Leigh I never thought you were such a deep person when I saw you. You seemed such a jolly and funny guy. "Sam people like me…people like Bruce, we want to forget some pieces of our lives, but those pieces turn up like a swords of a knight, never can be separated from him. In order to keep the tender side of the knight from the dragon named society, we have to put on the helmets of glory, and hide the scared little kid inside." Jenkins said. "It's okay Leigh, it's alright. But what happened. That made you so deep?" she asked. "Well, I am not a suspect to whom you are interrogating Sam. Let's say I am that London kid who is afraid of strange dark allies." Jenkins said with a slight smile. "You see that" Sam said pointing towards a hill with the `Hollywood` written on it. "So I am in real Hollywood now." He said. After a short drive they went to a building with the name `Prada` written. Leigh's Jaw was wide open. "Judging from your reaction, I deduce that you have never worn a Prada suit before." "How can I, they only sell to celebrities." Said Jenkins.

"Well I am on the verge of becoming one, but if you solve this one you will become a celeb too." Said Sam. They went inside and Sam saw a familiar face "Ryan!" she called and waved. A man with square head and a fine jaw line, with dusky brown eye balls came up towards them with a presidential walk. His walk made him look iconic and his blonde hair made him look like a king. "Hey Sam, here to shop for my party?" he asked. "Not for me." She said. "Oh right I see it now, you are inviting your boyfriend." Ryan said looking at Jenkins. "I bet Bruce is going to feel jealous." Said Ryan. Sam looked at the floor with her cheeks reddened. "Alright is that blush for Him or for Bruce?" asked Ryan. "Oh c'mon Ryan he is not my boyfriend." Said Sam. "More like friend from work. "said Jenkins. "Oh, fine anyway I was just kidding." Ryan said. He offered a shake hand to Jenkins and said, "Hope you don't mind dude, well my name is Ryan Johnson's" he said "Oh its totally fine sir, I am private detective Leigh Jenkins." Leigh said taking the hand shake. "Oh detective, then I would be pleased if you would show me your art of deduction." Said Ryan. "Well, if I start, I may go on till morning." Leigh said. "Oh then that would be a time, next time then detective." Ryan said. "Yes, meet you at the party, Ryan" said Jenkins. "Alright Leigh, it would be fun to have you, anyway, gotta run. See you later Sam and Leigh." Ryan said and rolled off. "So I guess you can help yourself for your outfit, and I will wait." Sam said. "Yes" said Jenkins. "The party will start after an hour, and our venue is just the terrace of this building." Said Sam. "Alright, then I will see you at the lift after half an hour." Leigh declared.

After an hour Leigh was seen in a Green Prada party tux near the lift and Sam came wearing a silver party gown. "Ready to rock a celeb party? Besides I can't wait to see Bruce." Sam said while Jenkins gave her a bit mischievous look "Well and ready to make some contacts that might help us in the case?" she asked. "I'm ready for both." Said Jenkins said. "Well we can have a bit fun while working on a case." She said "Well not a professional courtesy, but everything is okay when you are in Hollywood." Leigh said. Just then the elevator arrived with a ding sound. They both went in the elevator Sam pressed the button with `20` written on it. "So excited Leigh?" Sam asked "Excited and focused too." Leigh replied. After a short chat they arrived at the 20th floor, the door opened. Opposite the lift's door was a gate with automatic glass door, in front of which was standing a man in a black suit wearing black sunglasses and a Bluetooth device in his right ear, he was carrying steel knuckles in his right hand.

There were two guys on each side of the door armed with pistols. "Ma`am, may I know your name?" the man with sunglasses asked. "Samuleen Hawkins" said Sam the armed guy checked a stapled sheet in his hand "I am afraid there is no such name in the guest list ma`am." Said the man. "Well then check the name `Sam`" said Sam. "The guy checked the list again and said. "Well, there is, welcome Miss Sam." Said the guard. "Thanks, may we go in?" she asked. "Of course ma`am" the guard said, they both rolled in.

Inside there was a small orchestra being played in the right corner. In the left corner, was a small bar. In the front corner there was a glass covered room in which people were dancing duets. While in the center there was a disco ball attached to the ceiling, where people were dancing under it, and near it was a DJ. Jenkins could see many familiar faces from the movies and TV. There were waiters moving around serving refreshment drinks. Just then Ryan arrived on the scene with a man that probably stood 5`9 he was wearing a black Armani party tux a black bow tie and his walk was majestic. He had a clean face with blue eyes. "Bruce! Sam cried and hugged him. "Hey hey, easy there miss detective." Said Bruce. "Okay, wait Bruce, meet Leigh. Leigh, meet Bruce

Wilson. "Hey, Bruce so finally I met the person Sam was talking about all the time." Said Jenkins. "Oh, you told good about me right?" Bruce asked to Sam. "Well of course." Said Sam. She spotted a familiar guy with a golden tux and a French cut beard. "Why on earth have you invited Ruth to the party" Sam asked to Ryan. "I know I shouldn't have, but he has donated huge amount for the fundraiser, not only that, I have invited Serone too."Ryan said giving a guilty look. "After what they have done to you." Said Sam "Well, I aint talking to them, it's just for formality." Said Ryan. "Alright, your party anyway." Said Sam "Gentlemen, and milady, would you all like a drink in the ball room?" Bruce asked. "Yes of course" said Sam. "I`ll get Megan then" said Ryan. "What about you Leigh?" Bruce asked. "I think I`ll stick here. I don't have a partner to dance with." Said Jenkins. "I guess Halley could take care of that." Said Bruce and he called out for Halley. A woman in a blue dress came towards them. "Hey Bruce. Need any help" Halley said. "Well, not me but my mutual Leigh here needs someone to dance with, you okay to save the day?" Bruce asked. "Any of Bruce`s friend is my friend." said Halley. "In that case milady, may I have this dance?" Leigh asked "Sure Mr. Leigh." Halley said. They all proceeded to the ball room.  When a twelve year old girl spill a glass of water on Leigh`s shoes. "Oops" the girl said giving Leigh a sorry look. "I am so so sorry." The girl said. "Hey it's not a problem, milady I`ll wipe it off with my handkerchief. Hey aren't you the young Miss. Watson I`ve been hearing all about in London?" Leigh asked to the twelve year old girl. "Yes, actually I have played a student witch in two movies" Said the girl. "In that case miss Watson, may I have your autograph?" said Jenkins. She gave him a cute smile and an innocent look. "This is a dream; no one has asked me for an autograph, my class mates and friends all mock me by calling witch." She said."Well, Miss. Watson, miracles do take place, Today when I woke up, I never thought that I would get to dance with Miss Berry." Leigh said. "Thanks I guess, well I have to leave now, my mommy is waiting for me." Said the girl. "Good bye Miss. Watson." Leigh said by waving her a goodbye, she went doing the same. They all then went to the ball room.

The ball room was a magnificent place with a massive chandelier in the middle attached to the ceiling while four small chandeliers in the four corners. There was a fine waltz being played and couples were dancing duets in the hall,In the corner, there was another little bar. Sam and Bruce started dancing, who were followed by Jenkins and Halley. Ryan took a momentary glance and went to dance with Meghan. The ball room was beautified by couples, famous actor, actresses, and many more important people of the town. Leigh was dancing with Halley. She was a bit relaxed and Leigh was thinking about the situation in which he did a wrong step that would turn into an accident and injure Halley, so he was taking each and every step carefully. Just then Ryan said. "Attention Ladies and Gentlemen, The moon is out, so I will show you a modification that I`ve made in my pent house." He clicked a little button in his hand and the ceiling went all transparent. The shining white moon, the glittering colorful stars were visible in the night sky. The Waltz was resumed. All these things made the place look like heaven.

Suddenly! The lights went off, there was a sound of glass break, and everybody raced to the corners of the room, a pair of red glowing eyes entered the room from the broken glass, and suddenly the lights returned exposing the red eyed man, he was wearing a carbon steel mask with black color sprayed on it. The eyes were red hot; they were made of some kind of LED. The anger and hatred were visible in his eyes if one could feel it. "I am so sorry, ladies and gentlemen, to disturb this sweet little party. I won't be here for long, if you give me Blake Ruth."

The man said. "Leigh you recognize him?" Asked Sam. "Yeah, our masked murderer...the...the Hood." Said Leigh. "I am no murderer" The hood declared. He located Blake Ruth, and he started walking towards him with a devil`s stance. Blake Ruth was frozen on his feet. "You, you filthy little-." Said the hood walking towards him, in no time he rushed to him, caught his collar, Blake Ruth was staring directly in his eyes. He was frightened and speechless. The hood punched him in the face, he fell down, then the hood drew two batons which were hanging on his back, he clicked a button on handle of both the batons, they increased a bit started glowing in glittery red. He was about to hit Blake when Jenkins pounced on him, throwing him aside the batons fell nearby, Jenkins removed his L.A.P.D issued gun and aimed it towards him, "Stop right there or I`ll fire. " said Jenkins. "I am not scared!" the hood shouted. He put his palms in the directions of his batons, and they were just attracted to his hands, like there was some kind of magnets between his hand and the batons. He clicked the button and discharged one of the baton and threw it on Jenkins like a boomerang, it hit Leigh on his hand disarming him, the baton came in Hood`s hand. Sam had a clean shot, she fired and the bullet hit on the Hood`s head!

The bullet fell down crumpled and the hood`s helmet was unaffected. "What!" she said in shock. Hood rushed towards Blake. Just then the security guards arrived. He hit a chop on Blake`s neck and he fell unconscious. The guards came running towards them, Hood pointed his palms towards them, and an unbearable sound started coming out from his hands, the sound was so harsh that no one could bear it, everyone in the ball room fell unconscious.

The hood sprayed a gas on Ruth`s face. He woke up; hood grabbed him by the collar and dragged him to the window. Then he charged his batons, rotated a dial on the end of the handles, and started beating him. Each and every hit was delivering 120 volts of electricity in his body. He was crying like a wounded animal. All the pain was in his cries. "No, no." He was crying. While the Hood kept beating him. "Ahh, ehh, no...I be...beg you... ahh...stop." Cried Ruth. After a moment of infinite torture the Hood stopped. "Oh...god " Ruth said with a hush of relaxation. The hood put his hand on his helmet and removed it. "What! No...it...it can't be you." Said Ruth. The hood grabbed him by his collar picked him and went towards the broken window. "No, no you can't do this...no." said Ruth. The hood was staring in his eyes, seeing the horror but beyond that, his cruelness, blood thirstiness and greediness. He then held him out of the window, loosening his grip. "*Your soul will keep wandering between heaven and hell.*" The hood said, and then he threw him off.

`Run Leigh, run don't look back. Run!` said a woman. Leigh started to run through a dark alley. Suddenly! `Nowhere to hide... you little piece of -.` said a man carrying a chain saw with a blot of blood. Leigh started to run the opposite direction. The man started to chase him. `Come to papa, little piggy, papa wants to eat a ham. ` Said the man. `No! leave me, leave me.` said Leigh still running. He was running and running in the alley, running from the man, running from someone he couldn't outrun. `Ha ha ha, you think you can out run papa.` Suddenly his lace was untied and he fell down, he started to crawl but there was a wall behind him. He stopped and closed his eyes in horror. The man held the chain saw up, he pressed a button and the saw started. He was about to make a strike...and...

"Leigh! Leigh!...c`mon dude wake up" said Sam. He opened his eyes "Huh...wh...wh...where...a...aa...am...Ah...ah..I." Jenkins asked. "At Ryan`s party, why are you looking so weird. Don't you know what happened?" Sam asked.

"H...ha...h...ha...hood. W...wh...wh...wh...what ha...ha... hap..Happened?" he asked. "Hey, hey , hey, cool down okay, cool it down. Re-Lax." Said Sam "I...I...a...a...am... ck...ck...ck...cka...cool." Jenkins said and sighed. "Hey, man it's okay, it happens in shock. Don't be afraid." She said. "I am not afraid!" Leigh shouted. She was shocked. "I...a...a...am...sss..ss...sorry." he said and sighed again. "It's okay, it's alright." She put a hand on his shoulder and said. "Y...yee...ye...yes...th...th...th...thanks." He said. "I`ve called an ambulance and well, there is another murder on the hands of the hood." She said. Jenkins sighed. They heard an ambulance siren. "Come down we'll see the body." Sam said. Jenkins nodded.

Everybody was gathered around the body except Ryan, he was nowhere to be seen. Two cops arranged a `do not cross` tape within a radius around it. A woman wearing white lab coat and with a doctor`s tag came towards Leigh and Sam. She handed some pills to Jenkins. "Take them Leigh, you will feel better." Said Sam. "Yes son, take them." Said the woman in the lab coat. Jenkins sighed and took them. "Huh" he said. "Feeling any better?" the doctor asked. "A...a bit." He said. "It's okay." The doctor said. "O...Okay so what do we h...Have?" he asked. "Well, a mid forties Hollywood screen writer. Cause of death;

fracture in the skull due to falling from a great height. Multiple fractures in the body and multiple burning wounds, was tazored by some thing." Said the doctor. Jenkins took a deep breath. "Well, I am afraid he did not die of falling. You said that there was huge fracture in the head right. If it was the case then he would have fallen on his head. If he would have fallen on the head, then it should have crumpled, that's because he fell from the twentieth floor. But the head is still intact, except that swelling on his forehead and the small scratch on his head. The scratch is because of the glass piece of the broken window from which he was thrown, this is because I was fallen near the window, when Sam woke me up I noticed a small blood patch on the upper glass. If he would have fallen on his head doctor, then you would have got nothing but a crushed head. The conclusion, he died in mid air. His head was hit hard with the batons that the hood used. Resulting of cracking of his skull, but the blow was a bit bearable until the skull was cracking, I think before dying the man must have got a shock, not a physical shock obviously but a mental shock." He said. "Oh, you did not fumble." Said Sam. "I...I...u...usually don't while...de...de...deducing." He said. "Are you a bloody robot?" the doctor asked terrified. "I am n..No robot, I am just a sleuth of deductions." He said. "Since we know the cause of death and every other thing, let's pack this up." Said Sam. They placed the body in a white cover and carried it in the ambulance. Jenkins and Sam went to her car.

"You alright?" Asked Sam. "Ye...ye...yes." Jenkins answered. "Why are you fumbling?" She asked. "N... no...i...it is nothing." He answered. "If you feel tensed, just take those pills." She said. "Yes I am a...ab...absolutely fine. Ju...j...just need to ck...ck...clear my mind." He said. "Okay, just heads up when you clear y`er mind. I`ll drive." She said. Jenkins nodded. "Ck...ck...can you I...low...lower down the window?" he asked. "With pleasure." She said pushing down a button. The window lowered. Jenkins started to stare the long and glittering buildings. "This might sooth you more." Sam pushed the radio button unplugging it from the police wired communicator. A song started to play. `*There's a road I'd like to tell you about, lives in my home town.*` Jenkins smiled and said "That might help." The song continued to play `*Lake shore drive the road is called, and it'll take you up or down.*` Jenkins closed his eyes, with the sweet song in the background and the chill wind embracing his face he started to think. `*I am not a kid anymore, then why, why have the fumbles started again. I`ve taken therapies on that. Then why have* *they started again. I erased the memory of the alley long ago, then why does it keeps coming back to me? Am I not doing enough to forget all this? But why all the bad things happen to me? First Mother, Then Alex, Then Annie, Then Ben and then Andrew. Why do people I get closer to end up dead? Why? Is them being dead my fault? Yes it has to be. I have many enemies in London, but I have taken all the precautions of them not having any information about my personal life. So why people closer to me keep dying.`* Then a familiar face came in front of his eyes. `*why do I care for her so much, will she...will she end up dying too? And Mrs. Jonas. Will she also die. No, no why is this happening to me again, all of a sudden? Wait am I suffering with PTSD? No it can`t be, No not Gwen and Mrs.Jonas too.`* Jenkins` eyes were closed and the song just finished. He opened his eyes, took one of the pills. "Feeling better?" Sam asked. "Yeah...a...a bit." He answered. "If you are fine then listen, so I told T Malik, our techie at the Major crimes office to look into Tom Frank`s things, like his E-mails, his Bank account etcetera, etcetera." Said Sam "And what did he find?" Leigh asked. "Well, Tom was a very shady person. He had a secret E-mail Id on a very unusual website which I guess isn't used by common people. It's called *www.thetrident .com*, I am sad to say this but he extorted money." She said with a sad face. "You know,

Tom was like a father to me. When my mom and dad passed I was shifted to a foster home with Bruce for some days, I lived there for a while and Bruce went with his uncle. When I became a detective, I came in contact with Tom, and he was too kind to me. He treated me like his daughter. Now I come to know this." Said Sam. Tears were trembling down from her eyes. "You will be more shocked when you see this." she said handing him her cell phone, there was a text message saying mails in Tom`s Trident account. He handed her a handkerchief and started reading it. *Pegasus23@thetrident.com`, the stuff is received; the consignment is on its way. Your money will be transferred to your Swiss account.........Poseidon.`* "Well, this is going to go big." Said Jenkins. "That's not it, scroll down see the texts Tom`s received." She said and he scrolled down. *`Your money is transferred, now once the consignment is here we can start the business, soon trident shall rule Athens.....PN`* the message said. "This message is three months earlier. The email is too old; probably Tom would be in his early thirties that time. "said Jenkins. "Can you deduce anything from these?" she asked. "With pleasure. Tom`s username its Pegasus, Pegasus is the flying horse in the Greek mythology, the sender of these messages is called Poseidon. Well guess what, who is Pegasus` father in the Greek mythology?...its Poseidon.

Pegasus and Poseidon are code names. Poseidon is the leader of this drug business, drugs as he used the term `stuff` the alternative for drugs in the American under world. But their business is not only drugs; it's something bigger than this because of the word `consignment` it could be gold, weapons or something more dangerous, apart from Tom and this person calling himself Poseidon, there is a third person involved, because they are calling themselves the trident. There is something more interesting, the hood killed Tom, and then he kills Blake Ruth. "Said Jenkins. "Do you mean that Blake Ruth was involved with Tom in this trident business?" Sam asked. "Yes, it is." He declared. "Okay, I`ll tell T to dig in Blake." Said Sam. "Tell me how was Blake`s reputation in the Hollywood?" Jenkins asked "Not good, he was quite the dirty person. His dialogues consisted most curses, he was probably the second most hated guy here. "She said. "Who's the first?" Jenkins asked. "The fat white man with him in the party, Billy Serone, he`s the most hated, but everyone is scared of him he is quite the bully. He has produced many films with Blake Ruth as the script writer." She said," Not only that, he is a crime lord, we believe that he owns a criminal organization here in L.A, but every time we try to get him, we have to leave him because of lack of evidence." She said "I guess I will put him in after we deal with this Hood guy and the trident." Said Jenkins. "By the way, I was a bit confused and I drove us to Ryan`s house" She said by stopping the car. "Wait, the party one?" Jenkins asked. "No, his personal residence, that's just a place where he throws parties. I am going to be there at his place tonight, well Major crimes has given you Jimmy Marshall`s right?" she asked with a queer expression. "So, it is the worst lodge in Hollywood." He said "Yeah, that place is filled with all the shit in the world." Sam said. "Yeah, still no problem, I can find my way there." Jenkins said. "Oh hey, you can stay At Ryan`s with me.  I mean not exactly with me." She grinned. "Its alright I`ll go to Jimmy Marshall`s" Said Jenkins. "Oh c`Mon you are getting to stay at a Hollywood star's condo, then why are you being a jerk." Said Sam "Okay *gentille fille* if you insist." He said. They both went upstairs to Ryan`s house. They found Bruce hanging out there. The moment Bruce saw Sam, he went and hugged her. "Hey, it's okay, sometimes people aren't what we know they are." Said Bruce. "So you told him what T Malik found about Tom?" Jenkins asked. "Yeah, I texted him." She said. Just then Ryan emerged from inside with a bandage on his hand. "Hey Sam, hey... Leigh." He said. "Oh I have seen you aren't pleased to see me here." Said Jenkins. "Hey, no nothing like that, it's okay." Said Ryan. "Can he stay with us, they have given him Jimmy Marshall`s." said Sam "Oh, dude I`ll tell you, that place is total crap." Ryan said to Jenkins. "So, can he stay here tonight?" Sam asked. "Of course, would be my pleasure to have a Londoner." Said Ryan. "Well guys, I am shifting to London after my current shoot." Said Bruce. "You are?" Sam asked with a bit sad look. "Sam we have talked this over." Said Bruce. "Guys chill it out." Said Ryan. "Hey Ryan, when that psycho hood came to the ball room where were you, you weren't seen by any of us till the ambulance arrived, where were you, and what's with the wound on your hand?" Sam asked. "I...I...err..."

"I...err...I went to say goodbye to a very important guest" said Ryan. Jenkins closed his eyes recollected all the physical features of the hood, and then he fixed a momentary glance towards Ryan."What`s with your hand?" Jenkins asked. "I just cut myself out while peeling onions." Said Ryan. "A Hollywood shining star cuts onions himself? Well you come from the party to your house directly, without even informing anybody, even when the party became a crime scene? And you were peeling onion at night 10:30 said Jenkins. "Oh, c`mon Leigh, you seriously think that this guy is the hood, I mean I know this biggy wiggy harmless innocent infant from child hood, and mind you he can't even, kill an insect." Said Bruce pulling Ryan`s leg. "Hey, I massacred a whole damn anthill okay." Said Ryan. "Okay now I have to arrest you for the charges of mass destruction." Said Sam. "Hey, you can't do that to me, I am your crush`s best friend." Said Ryan. Sam gave him a questioning look. "Anyway, who is this hood guy though?" Ryan asked. Jenkins sharpened his ears and directly started to stare in Ryan`s eyes with an undercover smile on his face. His very own technique to identify criminals on the spot without them even knowing. "The one who killed our beloved Tom and Blake Ruth tonight." Said Bruce. "He did sound like Darth Vader though." Said Sam. "Well, how did that look?" Bruce asked. "Man, was it really like Darth Vader? Like Darth Vader, Darth Vader?" Ryan asked. "He used voice synthesizer." Said Sam. "A sweet move." Said Jenkins. "Well, enough guys, I think we should sleep now, remember Ryan, you've got a shoot tomorrow" said Bruce. "Yeah, you too." Said Ryan. "Right, let's go to sleep. We have work to do as well Leigh." Said Sam. "Right, hey Sam, before sleeping is T doing overnight?" Jenkins asked. "Yeah, I will tell him to dig in Blake Ruth." She said. They all went to sleep.

The next day. Leigh woke up to see that Ryan and Bruce were away for their respective shootings. Sam was waiting in the drawing room. He got ready and they started to Major crimes office. "So, You and Bruce huh?" asked Leigh. "What do I say; see I told you that I liked him from my childhood. So does he. All I want to do is give him a normal life. He keeps on saying that he misses his parents and uncle, he says that I and Ryan are his only family left." Said Sam. "I understand, it is not easy for him, to be honest, I feel him." Said Jenkins. "Wait yours too?" Sam asked. "Well, it's a bit complicated, at least Bruce has you two, his best friends." Said Jenkins. "Yeah, but he needs to settle, he is not well right now, he is psychologically a bit ill, I want to help him in every way I can." Said Sam. "Yeah, there must be too much pressure, but he never seems so in interviews." Said Jenkins. "He is a good actor." She said. "Winning three Oscars from last three years, he so is." Said Jenkins. "Yeah, well enough about me, tell me something about you." She asked. "To be very honest, I like a girl. Yeah, the problem is whomever I get close to, ends up dying. I don't want this to happen with her too." He said becoming a bit restless. She put her hand on his shoulder and eased him. "It's alright." She said. "Its unjust Leigh, you shouldn't think like this." she said. "Well, what's your say, Justice or vengeance?" He asked. "Both are peculiar things, Justice in some cases is partial or constrained. But vengeance, I believe might seem unethical but it can also be justice. Vengeance is unethical no doubt, but it comes in role when Justice fails to accomplish its purpose." Said Sam. "So what is it for you, Justice or vengeance?" Jenkins asked. "It's gotta be Justice, we live in a civilized world, we should behave like civilized people." She said. "What about you?" she asked. "My views on Justice and Vengeance are a bit complex. "Justice might be the clearer and brighter surface of the sea, but vengeance is the dark deep drowns, darker but clean." He said. "So it's Vengeance then?" she asked. "I might tell you that when the time is correct." He said. "When will it be?" she asked. "We will see." He said. "Yeah we will see." She said. "So what's with this guy Billy Serone?" he asked. "How many times are you gonna ask?" she said. "I will till I don't get satisfied." He said. "Alright alright, see I was on him from last three years, every time I got any proper evidence, they used to tamper it up. His people had infiltrated major crimes, but we cleaned it up a few months before. All I could know about Billy Johaanish Serone, is that he came to L.A years ago when I guess Bruce`s parents died, some months prior. He entered in the production business with a company named Neptune productions. But that's just a cover; he does all his main work underneath, drugs, extortions, trafficking, murders and many more. His origin is Russian I guess cause we don't know that, we think it might be because of his accent." She said. "I think I will help you catch him, after we deal with the hood." Said Jenkins. They approached a traffic signal, which instantly welcomed their arrival with a red light. Leigh`s gaze went to a wall, which had a poster on it saying. `Gonies kai daimones starring Tom Franks as Carlbert Stronton.` And in the end it was written `Neptune productions.` "So Tom did Greek films too?" Jenkins asked. "Oh no it was just a charity production for Greek refugees here, but that got canceled, Tom said he didn't want to work for a producer like Serone. But now I guess it might be that they both were business rivals." She said. "Fascinating very, very fascinating." Said Jenkins. The light was still red. "Oh screw this." said Sam pressing a button that started the siren, they rolled off.

At major crimes office, Jenkins saw a man with an afro hair style running towards them, "C`mon man, you told me to put a hit Shaw on Ruth, I found something really good." Said the man. "Thanks T, let's see what we got from Blake Ruth." Said Sam. They went to their techs section. T handed Sam some sheets of stapled paper.

"God! That means Tom was working with Blake Ruth." She said handing the papers to Jenkins. He saw the papers. `Pegasus has been informed, his deeds are satisfied, now the time to act is yours Arion. Do not disappoint Poseidon.............PN.` the message said. Leigh turned the page. `Arion301@thetrident.com I am proud of you Arion. Now the city of Athens is Poseidon`s......PN. ` He turned the page. `Arion, our existence is in deep trouble, the antitheos have got information we must burn them.......... PN.` Jenkins turned the page `My son Arion I am proud, we have burned our enemies to ashes. Now the only challenge is the antitheos in the pouli.............PN.` He handed the sheets back to T. "Fascinating very, very fascinating." Said Jenkins. "That so damn unbelievable, Ruth Okay, but Tom now seems like the guy whom I never knew." Said Sam "It's okay Sam" said T. "Truth is the poison as well as the honeydew." Said Jenkins. "What do we do now?" she asked. "Who was the person closest to Blake Ruth?" Jenkins cross-questioned. "I am afraid that's Billy Serone." Said T. "What are we waiting for?" Leigh asked. "Woah woah woah, wait, British boy, this is The Billy Serone we`re talkin about." Said T. "Where is he right now?" T asked. "In his creepy production house, obviously." Said Sam. "Let's go then." Jenkins announced. "Hey Sam, can I go home, I was working overnight and I have got a date." Said T. "Yeah I`ll issue you a leave, just inform Cap Bolt before going." Said Sam. T gave a smile; Jenkins saw notoriousness in his eyes. "When you come back, just start digging up on Billy." Said Sam. "Yes" he said and ran off to captain Bolt`s office. Leigh and Sam went to her car.

"So now will you show me the sheet you tore off?" Leigh said gently. Sam sighed a bit and said, "Okay, here it is." Here it is. She handed him the sheet he started reading. `Arion, Pegasus and your boss Poseidon I am aware with all your deeds, soon you shall be punished...............RJ.` "You really think that it might be Ryan?" Jenkins asked. "Why can't he be, three days ago Tom was an innocent guy who believed in non violence." She said. "Why are you relieved, you believe too?" she asked. "Well, Ryan........I had my suspicions." Said Jenkins. "Watch out for people in the major crimes too." Said Jenkins. "What!" she said. "Nothing like that, just watch out." Said Jenkins."Okay," she said with a questioning look.

They started for Billy`s production house. "So where is the house?" Jenkins asked "Its beside the docks near the old ghetto." She answered. "Shouldn't a production house be in the middle of the city?" Said Jenkins. "This is Billy Serone we`re talking about." Said Sam "Fascinating very, very fascinating." Said Jenkins. "Well Sam?" he said "Um hmm" she said. "Bruce has quite the talent, he is Jo Wilson`s son right?" Jenkins asked "Oh, no he has nothing to do with Jo Wilson, though Jo Wilson died in an accident too. All Bruce`s relatives and parents were journalists or news reporters." Said Sam. By the time they arrived Serone`s production house, the sun had started to set.

They entered Billy`s production house, there was a weird smell in the air that Jenkins sensed. They knocked the main door and came towards the receptionist. "We are from L.A.P.D. we have some questions for Mr. Serone." Sam said to the receptionist. "He is right in the main room listening to script." Said the receptionist.

Leigh and Sam dashed opened the door of main room, "Not you again?" Said a fat man wearing a white three piece suit, had a black grey beard, a bit of hair on his head, his eyes were blue and swollen, he removed a cigar from his mouth and gave it to a blonde woman wearing red dress. The woman took a puff and kept it in the ashtray. "Yeah Me, we want to question you once again so come here fast and we won't torture you much to get our answers." Said Sam. "Hey you, play it cool or I will fry and eat you off." Said Billy Serone. Jenkins who was standing behind her, came forth and showed his presence. Serone was a bit surprised, and so was Jenkins. "Do I know you detective?" Serone asked. "I don't think so" said Jenkins. "Alright Serone we have questions for ya" said Sam. "This is the last time you will be asking me questions." Said Serone. "So, what do you know about Blake Ruth?" she asked. "Not here gorgie, in the yard." He said. She frowned and said "Whatever." They headed to his yard.

The yard was well maintained, short conifers in the corners. On one side of the yard was the sea and on the other side was a huge building which lead to an alley way. It was almost dark when they came. The office door was guarded by two bouncers or henchmen, to be called. Near the sea, there was a roofed shack with chairs and a table. They went towards it and sat on the chairs. Jenkins sat on the chair behind such that the wall was visible, beyond which there were the mighty waters and the henchmen were also visible from his chair. Sam sat opposite to Jenkins; all she could see was his face, and the horizon beyond. Serone sat adjacent to both, he could see the sea.

"So Mr. Serone, do you know anything about Tom Franks?" Sam asked. "Ahh Tom Franks, see I was really a fan of his acting, I even offered him a role, he agreed. We shot it half, then suddenly he turned the role down, after that I was in no contact with him. The last I heard about him was he was murdered by that crazy masked man" said Serone. Jenkins just looked at the men near the gate, they were fallen unconscious. "You talking about me possie?" a synthesized voice came from near the walls. There he was standing on the wall, wearing the mask. With the red eyes glowing and his red hot charged batons in his hand. He threw a little ball on the floor of the shack, it rolled near Sam. "No!" Jenkins shouted and pounced on Sam. They both rolled down on the land. The ball instead of exploding, released a gas. Serone started to cough. The hood uncharged one baton and hanged it on his back. He jumped in the shack, and punched hard on Serone`s face, he landed down the shack. He stood up trembling and started running towards the gate. Sam and Leigh rose up; both of them removed their respective pistols and pointed at him."Throw your weapons and kneel down, you psycho" She ordered. "You fools!" he said in his haunting synthesized voice. Serone almost reached the gate, "Throw your weapons" Said Sam. "Okay if that's your choice" said the Hood, he uncharged the baton and threw it at their hands it hit their hands and disarmed them. The baton returned in his hand.

He jumped over them with a summer Sault like a ninja and started running towards Serone. Serone reached towards the gate beside his unconscious henchmen. The door was locked with something sticky. He tried opening it, which it wasn't. He woke his guards up. "You, come with me, and you take care of them." Said Serone to both of them. Then he started running towards the alley way with one of the guards. The other aimed a pistol towards the charging hood. He was about to fire when hood threw his boomerang baton towards him, it hit him and at the same time he fired, the bullet was deflected it shot Jenkins above the elbow. "No!" the hood shouted. The henchman fell down while Serone rolled off in the alley. The hood first looked at Jenkins then at Sam. Then he started running behind Serone. Sam raced towards Leigh. "Your arm" she said. "I am fine, you go catch the hood." He said. "No, you are hurt." She said. "Just go I am right behind!" he shouted. Sam went inside the alley.

While Serone reached on the other side of the alley, there was a limousine waiting for him. He sat in and it rolled off. On the other side, Jenkins put his right hand on his left hand, covering the wound and advanced to the alley. He went inside the dark alley, and instantly fell on his knees. A familiar memory started playing in front of his eyes.

`Run Leigh, run don't look back. Run!` said a woman. Leigh started to run through a dark alley. Suddenly! `Nowhere to hide... you little piece of shit.` said a man carrying a chain saw with a blot of blood. Leigh started to run the opposite direction. The man started to chase him. `Come to papa, little piggy, papa wants to eat a ham.` said the man. `No! leave me, leave me.` said Leigh still running. He was running and running in the alley, running from the man, running from someone he couldn't outrun. `Ha ha ha, you think you can out run papa.` Suddenly his lace was untied and he fell down, he started to crawl but there was a wall behind him. He stopped and closed his eyes in horror. The man held the chain saw up, he pressed a button and the saw started. He was about to make a strike...and...

Serone`s henchman came towards him, he was standing behind the knelt down Leigh, who was in his own state of horror. He pointed the gun on Leigh`s head. His finger was about to embrace the trigger. Suddenly! A baton appeared from the darkness and hit hard on the head of the henchman. He went down instantly. The baton too fell down. The hood emerged from the shadows. He walked towards Jenkins, and picked up his baton. While Jenkins collapsed on the ground falling unconscious. "I am no murderer" The hood said, and disappeared.

Leigh Jenkins was walking in a grave yard. It was night; two street lights each on the corner were just the two elements emitting an enormously little amount of light. The wind was blowing quiet soothingly and there were cries of dogs audible. There was a dead tree in the center of the grave yard, on which a raven was sitting brushing its beak against the bark. Jenkins walked straight to the tree, he wasn't able to walk properly. Something was wrong with his right knee. He was using a walking stick. He went near a grave and glanced it. `Been a long time eh?` he said and resumed walking pass it. On the tombstone it was written `Here Lies Benjamin steel may his soul Rest in Peace.` Jenkins kept walking straight when another tombstone appeared in front of him. `Do you feel you`re brought to justice?` on the tombstone of this grave the name was `Annie Skarts` he walked past the grave and went to another one. He pulled out a rose from the top pocket of his overcoat and placed it beside the tombstone. A drop of tear trembled down his eye and fell on the rose. On the tombstone it was inscribed `Gwendolyn Radcliffe.`

"Oh My God" Leigh woke up. He found himself and Sam in an ambulance."Bad dream?" Sam asked. "Nightmare!"

he said. "Where are we? What happened?" Serone got off. The hood tried to terminate him when we were questioning him." Said Sam. "I know that part, tell me what happened next?" he asked. "We were chasing the hood and Serone in an alley where you I guess lost your senses. I went behind Serone, he got off, and you might owe the hood your life." She said handing him a LCD display device. Jenkins saw the footage of how the hood saved him in the alley. "I...I don't understand. Why would he save you instead of letting you die? No offense by the way." She said. "None taken. We know something for sure that the third guy we are finding is Serone himself. The hood first kills Tom who was called Pegasus in the trident and then takes down Ruth who was called Arion. Then he goes behind Serone." He said. "True that is." Said Sam. "What should be our next move?" Sam asked. "First of all give me a map of Hollywood, I want to see all the alley ways in this city." He said. "Whoa! Are you crazy? To by heart the complete map you might require decades." She said. "Well I`m Leigh Jenkins and nothing is impossible for me." He said. "Cool down Mr. Photographicbrains." She said. "Its Jenkins, Leigh Jenkins." He said. Sam handed him a map. "Take this but I don't think you can really know all the places in this city. It'll take too long." She said. "I by hearted the whole London in one minute twenty five seconds then Hollywood isn't a big deal. People call me more to ask routes rather than to investigate something." He declared. "Dude you really are crazy." She said with a smile. "I`m not crazy, my brain is just nimble witty extraordinarily brilliantly genius." He said. "Alright Mr. Adjectives, what's our next move." She asked. "Hey don't call me that you bothersome annoying name giving girl." He said. "See" she said bursting out laughing. "Whatever" he said annoyingly. "Well I wonder what does Ryan`s parents do?" he asked. "Oh Ryan`s mum was a news reporter, his father was a script writer." She said. "What about Bruce`s parents? Jenkins asked. She saddened a bit and said "Both of them were journalists." She said. "Enough of chit chat, what we do now?" she asked. "You told T to dig in Serone`s right?" he asked. "Well he did pretty well; we found evidences about his drug business. One thing, he was supposed to receive a consignment today at nine. But that was cancelled." She said. "Now that's what you call perfect luck" said Jenkins. "Care to elaborate?" she said. "Alright, now we send Serone a fake message that the consignment is going to come. We bring him to the abandoned water purification factory. You will take two, only two officers to the factory, you ambush him there and arrest both, hood who has to come there to take his failed shot."

Said Jenkins. "Why only two? How do you know for sure that the hood will come there? And what are you gonna do?" she asked. "See, the hood is well aware of Serone`s whereabouts, there is no nice place like the abandoned factory to finish the work. If you go there with an entire force the enemies will be alert, and if I am right Serone will just bring one or two of his thugs with him." He said. "You didn't tell me what you are going to do?" she asked. "There is something I need to know, it's best if I do this alone. If I am right then we will have Serone and the hood both tonight. One more thing can you give me your car, you can borrow someone else's" he said. "She handed him the keys with a sigh. He took them and ran towards the door. "Leigh!" she said. He turned his head towards her. "How do you know you are right, gut feeling?" she asked. "Nope miss....I am always right." He said and ran down. She gave a smile. On the stairs Jenkins almost collided with somebody. "Ryan? What are you doing here?" Jenkins asked "Oh uh...well...I was here to see Sam." Ryan said. "Okay" said Jenkins. "But where are you going in such a hurry?" Ryan asked. "I have some work, well we are going to take down Serone in the abandoned water factory tonight at nine" said Jenkins. "That's pretty awesome." Ryan said and Jenkins ran down. `What an Idiot." Ryan said to himself.

"Alright, Jim and Harvey, finish off your work till eight, we are going to bust the hood and our favorite Serone." Sam said. Both the cops nodded. Just then Ryan showed up. "We need to talk Ryan!" Sam said in a stubborn voice. "What's it? Why so serious?" Ryan asked. "Cut it, I will come to your house when I finish this hood and Serone business once and for all." She said. "Y...ye... yeah" Ryan said.

Leigh was in a telephone booth near a cyber cafe. "Goldenlod, it's me Leigh, look I need you to mail me something...yeah, when I was there. One more thing, You remember I told you about that apparent plane crash... yeah, I think I might solve that too...thanks for your help Goldie, probably you will see me in tomorrow`s news. "He said and went in the cyber café. He logged in his mail ID, and saw a mail from Victor Igor Goldenlod. He opened it. "Hmm, fascinating very, very fascinating." He said. He printed something, paid the café owner. Folded the printed sheet and kept it in his pocket and went out. By the time it was eight o clock.

"Jim, Harvey come on we`ve got some criminals to catch, one of them to be killed." Sam said with a determined smile. They started for the factory. While Jenkins went to an archive of news and reports. There wasn't anybody there it was dark and possibly abandoned."Boy, Americans really don't know the value of documents do they?" he asked to himself. He started finding the compartment `J` It was a bit dark so it was being difficult for him.

Sam, Harvey and Jim reached the back gate of the factory "Alright I`ll take the back gate you two take the front gate, stay hidden and sharp, maintain radio contact in every five minutes. We will wait till Leigh arrives then we roll in." Sam ordered. "Yes ma`am" said the both of them. They silently came out of the car. Sam hooked her radio on her belt and pulled out her gun from the holster, she rushed beside a bush, from where the back gate was visible. The two officers tiptoed to the front gate and hid behind a big garbage box ."Is that Ryan`s car?" Jim said pointing to a green stingray near the bushes. "Might be, what do we gotta do with that." Said Harvey "Yeah man" said Jim and unhooked his radio "Sam, this is Jim, come in?" said Jim. Sam unhooked her radio pressed the mic button and said. "Jim I read you, now stay silent and sharp, keep reporting." Jim pressed the mic button and said "Yes Sam, over and out". Just then a cell phone in Sam`s jeans pocket buzzed. She took it out, there was a message she read it `I am almost there, have you arrived with the consignment............B.S` she started typing

`Yes, come in the tank hall and leave your men behind ` she clicked the `send` button. The phone buzzed again. `One stays out, the other comes in` she read and started typing `Okay, only one comes in` and kept the phone in her pocket. "Sam, you copy" Jim said on the radio. "Yeah copy, what's the status?" she said. "A Rolls Royce has arrived, there's Serone and two people out, Serone told one of them to stay out, he is heading with the other inside the factory, the gate guard is unarmed, the other carries a pistol, over" said Jim. Just then Sam saw the hood entering the factory from the back gate. "I copy, here`s the murderer, they might take time to find each other, we wait till Leigh arrives, you both take out the unarmed guy when I say and ascend to the tank hall, I will enter from here with Leigh, then we will bust both of them. Over and out. "She said. The guard on the front was whistling around. Sam crouched through the bushes till the glass of the tank hall. Serone entered the room "Where is the guy, where is ma money" he said in a bit Russian kind of accent. A baton came flying towards the armed guard and hit his chest.

Leigh came in the major crimes office and went straight to Bolt`s cabin. In the factory, the baton hit the guard on the chest, he fell unconscious. "What, no you crossed me" said serone, The hood emerged from the dark. `where are you Leigh, where are you` Sam whispered. The hood hit a hard punch on Serone`s face, he fell down. "where are you Leigh." She whispered. The hood picked him up by his collar, he took a breath "Today, you join your filthy friends." Said the hood in his horrifying synthesized voice. He picked his baton and clicked a button on the handle, it charged. He threw serone in a water tank and started ascending. `I can't wait anymore` Sam whispered, she unhooked her radio and said "Jim, Harvey roll in" on the front side Jim and Harvey exposed themselves and pointed their guns on the guard. "L.A.PD, put your hands behind your head and kneel down" said Jim. The guard instantly removed his pistol from the jacket and shot Jim on the shoulder and Harvey on his arm. Both fell unconscious. The guard looked behind and saw a log hit his face, he embraced the ground.

"How the hell you cross me?" Serone asked. Sam broke the glass rolling in "Hey pretty boy, I double crossed you both." She said taking out her pistol and aimed it on the hood. "You are such a fool" the hood said in his synthesized voice." Serone removed his small revolver and pointed it on Sam. "Yeah yeah, now leave you irritating hot, pain in my butt American you have no business" said

Serone. The hood removed a baton and pointed it on Serone, "You are going down anyway" he said. "No you both are going down" Said Sam and pressed the trigger, the bullet directly hit the hood on the right eye of his mask, he dropped his baton; Sam rolled and grabbed the baton. As a reflex Serone fired on Sam, but he missed and the bullet hit on a large cylinder behind Sam`s initial position, there was a hole in the cylinder and a gas stream started coming out. she charged the baton and hit it on the hood`s right eye where the bullet had been shot, that part of the mask cracked and fell down exposing the right eye of the hood. "You fool" he said."Yeah, kill that freak" said Serone. Sam pointed the gun to Serone. "What! No you -" he said.

"Alright this place is filled with highly combustible purification substances, so the last thing I would prefer to do here is playing with high voltage electric toys or guns" a voice came from the broken glass, Leigh Jenkins rose from the dark yard, and took out two big revolvers from his overcoat pockets, pointing one on Serone and other on the hood" Consider that statement as a pun..I..I mean as an Irony, God am bad with figure of speech" said Jenkins."So you finally showed up" said Sam "Oh, hey Sam, didn't see you there" said Jenkins. "Take him down detective, he is the murderer." Said Serone. Leigh turned the other revolver on Serone. "Yeah, you get him, I got the hood." Said Sam. "No wait" said Jenkins. "You idiots it's going to cost you. Do you even know who am I" said Serone. "Oh yes I am very well aware of who you are Serone, or may I call you Poseidon Nikolaou" said Jenkins. "At least someone has brains here." The hood said."What's going on Leigh?" Sam asked. "Relax; I am here to reveal everything." He said. "Talk" said Sam. Jenkins took a deep breath

"When we visited Serone`s house, I was amused by his look, he looked very similar to a criminal with whom I dealt with, long ago in Greece. He was first a crime lord in Greece, his name is Poseidon Nikolaou, I caught him for drug smuggling, child trafficking and many other charges. I handed him over to Greek police long ago. It was quiet impossible for me to believe that Serone was Poseidon all this time, I wasn't updated that Poseidon had broke through the Greek prison. But still Serone doesn't completely look like Poseidon. That is because he went under a plastic surgery in Athens. I could know this because I asked my friend to hack into the surgeon`s computer who operated you. Clearly I didn't have any doubts on him until I came around facts, his username in all the messages and even in the trident is Poseidon. Well this isn't a coincident; clearly you have a very poor imagination Poseidon. The second thing that made me think that Serone is Poseidon, is that the code names of your two henchmen, Tom Franks who was called as Pegasus, the son of Poseidon in the Greek Mythology, and Blake Ruth who was called Arion, the brother of Pegasus, and your statement, possie that never changed from last time we met, you used the term Athens for Hollywood, clearly couldn't you pick up some different names." He said and removed the printed sheets from his pocket, on one was the real face of Poseidon Nikolaou, and on the other were the details of his plastic surgery, the transformation of Poseidon Nikolaou to Billy Serone. "That's brilliant, now let's just take em both and finish this matter." Said Sam. "I am afraid we have to finish everything up here itself, Sam there is a reason I told you to bring both of them here. Now listen carefully Sam. There are many tragedies in this world, some are already there in your life, it's the job of that person to suffer those tragedies, but there are tragedies too that are mixed in your life, and it is the duty of that person to avenge himself from those unwanted tragedies. All this time I had different conceptions about the hood, for some time I even thought that T Malik was the hood.

But here I am resting with the truth in my hands. When you told me that Ryan`s mother was a news reporter, and Both of Bruce`s parents were Journalists, it all became clear to me. You might wonder why I was late here, I arranged Poseidon's photos first, then I went to an archive, an archive of journal researches, I was hoping to find something else, but I found something else. The key, the key that opens The vigilante The Hood`s true identity. It was nothing more peculiar than a piece of research paper of two journalists, three perhaps. Where two of them were killed in a car accident. But this wasn't a car accident. It was a well planned, well executed murder. A murder of two journalists who were going to be a threat to L.A`s new crime lord Billy Serone. Yes that evening five years ago When Bruce Wilson`s parents Brandon Wilson and Kelly Wilson died in the car crash. Let me bring the truth, it was no car crash, they were killed, they were silenced, by none other than Billy Serone or Poseidon Nikolaou. But he did not know about Adrian Wilson, the man who took their research and was going to bring it to London to me, but the plane crashed, and he died too, but the crash wasn't natural, it was planned. The plane crash was planned, there were explosives boarded in the plane. I identified this, because when a plane crashes it normally has its skeleton, but this one just exploded in mid air, and the debris landed on Spain, how strange, and Billy Serone was definitely involved in it because the debris had acetate peroxide and just a day before that a large amount of acetate peroxide was stolen from L.A chemical research laboratory, who was the most capable man of doing such thing none other than Billy Serone. But why would Billy Serone kill all these three people, the solution is simple, the couple first discovered about the shady business run by the trident they were going to expose the trident, so the trident decide to kill them off. They discovered that the couple`s research was given to Adrian Wilson who also suspected that Billy is Poseidon. This is why he was coming to London, he actually wrote an E-mail about all this to me, but when I checked it, it was too late. The thoughts of Ryan being the hood directly left my mind. This is just another common tale of tragedy, only difference here is that the victim instead of sitting crying chooses to step up and act. When Brandon Wilson, Kelly Wilson and Adrian Wilson are killed there is only one person that suffers all the pain, and that is none other than Bruce Wilson." He said.

"No, no it is not true. This cannot be true in a million years" Said Sam with tears in her eyes. "Sam, its okay" Said Leigh. "It is just not possible" said Sam. The hood dropped the baton. He put his arm on the chin part of the mask and other on the head, slightly he pulled the mask off, and it slipped from his hand. There he was all the time hiding, a mask behind a mask. "I really am the hood" Said Bruce. Serone was staring at three of them. "I am sorry Sam" said Bruce with tears in his eyes. "I have betrayed you and I am not trust worthy anymore. "He said with the tears falling down. "Arrest me" said Bruce. Sam`s eyes were reddened and tearful, "I...I...was ordered to shoot you on sight" she said. "So be it" Said Bruce. She aimed the gun on his forehead. Then she was about to pull the trigger. "You know that I love you, always" Bruce said. "I love you too" she said and was almost going to pull it.

"Stop!" Leigh shouted. "Before you decide to pull the trigger Sam, I want to say something" he said. "What?" both of them said together "Sam, I know, I know you consider vengeance uncivilized. I know you think it as ugly. You consider Justice to be more superior. Now is the time Sam, vengeance and justice do not walk parallelly, they both might have differences, but one point comes where Justice truly fails and that's where vengeance has to rise. In my case Justice did not fail. But in Bruce`s case justice has failed, this is why he had to take justice in his own hands and make it vengeance. When Bruce kills Tom, Ruth all the people whom they have extorted or treated badly are avenged. Sam there is no murderer here, only a man seeking peace in his destroyed state of mind. A man wanting to heal his scars. I don't see any killer here" he said. She lowered down her gun. "No, there has to be balance of Justice Leigh, They destroyed many innocent lives including my own, I brought them to Justice, and now I should be brought to justice." He said bringing his hands to Jenkins and pointing to the cuffs on Sam`s belt. "There is something I`ve learnt, Balance has to be there in every single thing that exists, but here, justice can be left unbalanced." He said. "But Leigh Jenkins never fails, he always gets the solution" said Bruce. "The solution to the three serial killings of Tom Franks, Blake Ruth and Billy Serone is that they were all murdered by a hired assassin named the hood, who was killed in the fatal explosion in the water purification factory." He said. Bruce picked up the mask wore it and went towards Serone. He grabbed him by the collar picked him, and then he threw him in the water tank. He came near Serone and charged his baton. "No, no no" said Serone he came towards "Yor soul will keep wandering between heaven and hell" the hood said and dipped the baton in the tank. "Aaahhh........" Serone cried.

He came towards Jenkins , removed the mask and handed it to him. Jenkins removed his revolver, "Listen Sam, two of your men are fallen unconscious near the front gate, I want you both to take them in the car." He said and kept the mask in the tank in the water near Serone`s body. "I will now shoot that cylindrical container, then we got three minutes till the whole place explodes. You both go and put the officers in the car. I will count till seventy, then shoot the cylinder and come out. Now go." He said. Both of them rushed out. Jenkins closed his eyes. `Mother, I miss you. I really do, the way dad treated you and me I`ve been trying to forget it all, but that time in the alley when he killed you in front of me, I am not able to forget that, I think this is why I have a phobia to dark alleys, hope one day I would be able to forget that all, but I will never forget you, never in a million years, I love you mom` he opened his eyes aimed his revolver and shot on the cylinder, a stream of gas rushed out of it. Three minutes later. The whole factory exploded.

"And now we welcome the Detective Mr. Leigh Charles Jenkins to come and say what exactly happened yesterday." Said Captain Holt. Leigh went towards the podium, adjusted the mike and said "We lured Poseidon Nikolaou and the hood in that factory thinking that it was deserted, when we rolled in they saw us and two of us were shot, one on the shoulder and the other on the thigh, so basically hood was hired to kill these three guys, well ,maybe some business rivalry, as earlier Sam said that these three were the part of criminal organization called trident. Well I am happy that the true guilty were exposed. All that is left of the hood is this; Jenkins showed a broken piece of mask with blood spots on it," forensics say that this blood doesn't belong to Serone, his body was found but the hood was completely destroyed." He said.

LAX airport, "Bruce, Sam, May you both find peace, and all the best for your life ahead." Said Jenkins, he hugged Sam then Bruce. "Thank you Leigh" said Bruce. "It isn't needed Bruce, take care and keep acting" said Leigh. "I will look forward to that moment when we work together another time" said Sam "So will I" said Leigh and boarded his flight.

Leigh took out a notepad from his bag and started to scribble on it.

Dear Mr. Adrian Wilson

 I think I finally have an answer to your E-mail, I will start with an apology, I should have seen your E-mail sooner and your grandson wouldn't have to go through all of that. The guilty ones are brought to justice, not by the way you wanted but Justice is served. Perhaps I have now understood that justice can change its medium anytime, in my case it was the law but in Bruce's case it wasn't. getting Justice served through the law wasn't Justice after all, and for people like Tom, Blake and Serone well, Nikolaou, the law is nothing more than a dominatable insect. They can use their power to snap out of it, I regret that I had to announce the death of the hood, but I did what I thought was correct at that time. Perhaps keeping the hood alive and exposing all three of them would have been better, as people like them could have started to fear at least someone. Thank you.

Yours truly

Leigh Jenkins

The flight landed at London international airport. Leigh came out of the airport, he saw a dustbin. He folded the paper gently and placed it on the dustbin, he took a deep breath, "Ahh, nothing is fresher than home." He said.

EPILOGUE

Leigh Jenkins was walking in a grave yard. It was night; two street lights each on the corner were just the two elements emitting an enormously little amount of light. The wind was blowing quiet soothingly and there were cries of dogs audible. There was a dead tree in the center of the grave yard, on which a raven was sitting brushing its beak against the bark. Jenkins walked straight to the tree. He went near a grave and glanced it. `Been a long time eh?` he said and resumed walking pass it. On the tombstone it was written `Here Lies Benjamin steel may his soul Rest in Peace. ` Jenkins kept walking straight when another tombstone appeared in front of him. `I know I did the right thing by not killing him` on the tombstone of this grave the name written was `Annie Skarts` he walked past the grave and went to another one. He placed a bouquet he was carrying, beside the tombstone. A drop of tear trembled down his eye and fell on the bouquet. `I miss you` he said. On this tombstone the name inscribed was `Emily Jenkins`

Leigh Jenkins:Volume 1

The End

By:- Atharva Joshi 'ARjun'.

www.ingramcontent.com/pod-product-compliance
Lightning Source LLC
LaVergne TN
LVHW091516170726

843492LV00001B/486